m.P.
9/3/2017

TIME'S A-WASTIN'!

Clemens opened his eyes.

Fargo said, "Last chance to tell me who is behind this."

"Go . . . to . . . hell."

"I'll find out anyway," Fargo said. "I'm going on to Meridian." Odds were whoever didn't want him there would make themselves known.

"Tried to . . . help . . . pard," Clemens managed to get out as more blood oozed.

"I still need a name."

Clemens didn't answer.

Standing, Fargo aimed his Colt at the center of Clemens's forehead. "Reckon I'll put you out of your misery, then."

For the first time fear showed in the other's eyes. "You said . . . you'd wait . . . and bury me."

"I said I'd bury you," Fargo agreed. "I never said I'd wait around for you to die."

"Bastard."

"Nice meeting you, too." Fargo stroked the trigger.

D0951181

THE
TRAILSMAN
#377

BOUNTY
HUNT

by

Jon Sharpe

WITHDRAWN

A SIGNET BOOK

SIGNET
Published by New American Library, a division of
Penguin Group (USA) Inc., 375 Hudson Street,
New York, New York 10014, USA
Penguin Group (Canada), 90 Eglinton Avenue East, Suite 700, Toronto,
Ontario M4P 2Y3, Canada (a division of Pearson Penguin Canada Inc.)
Penguin Books Ltd., 80 Strand, London WC2R 0RL, England
Penguin Ireland, 25 St. Stephen's Green, Dublin 2,
Ireland (a division of Penguin Books Ltd.)
Penguin Group (Australia), 707 Collins Street, Melbourne, Victoria 3008,
Australia (a division of Pearson Australia Group Pty. Ltd.)
Penguin Books India Pvt. Ltd., 11 Community Centre, Panchsheel Park,
New Delhi - 110 017, India
Penguin Group (NZ), 67 Apollo Drive, Rosedale, Auckland 0632,
New Zealand (a division of Pearson New Zealand Ltd.)
Penguin Books, Rosebank Office Park, 181 Jan Smuts Avenue,
Parktown North 2193, South Africa
Penguin China, B7 Jaiming Center, 27 East Third Ring Road North,
Chaoyang District, Beijing 100020, China

Penguin Books Ltd., Registered Offices:
80 Strand, London WC2R 0RL, England

First published by Signet, an imprint of New American Library,
a division of Penguin Group (USA) Inc.

First Printing, March 2013
10   9   8   7   6   5   4   3   2   1

The first chapter of this book previously appeared in *New Mexico Madman*, the three
hundred seventy-sixth volume in this series.

Copyright © Penguin Group (USA) Inc., 2013
All rights reserved. No part of this book may be reproduced, scanned, or distrib-
uted in any printed or electronic form without permission. Please do not partici-
pate in or encourage piracy of copyrighted materials in violation of the author's
rights. Purchase only authorized editions.

 REGISTERED TRADEMARK—MARCA REGISTRADA

Printed in the United States of America

PUBLISHER'S NOTE
This is a work of fiction. Names, characters, places, and incidents either are the
product of the author's imagination or are used fictitiously, and any resemblance to
actual persons, living or dead, business establishments, events, or locales is entirely
coincidental.

    The publisher does not have any control over and does not assume any respon-
sibility for author or third-party Web sites or their content.

If you purchased this book without a cover you should be aware that this book is
stolen property. It was reported as "unsold and destroyed" to the publisher and
neither the author nor the publisher has received any payment for this "stripped
book."

The Trailsman

Beginnings . . . they bend the tree and they mark the man. Skye Fargo was born when he was eighteen. Terror was his midwife, vengeance his first cry. Killing spawned Skye Fargo, ruthless, cold-blooded murder. Out of the acrid smoke of gunpowder still hanging in the air, he rose, cried out a promise never forgotten.

The Trailsman they began to call him all across the West: searcher, scout, hunter, the man who could see where others only looked, his skills for hire but not his soul, the man who lived each day to the fullest, yet trailed each tomorrow. Skye Fargo, the Trailsman, the seeker who could take the wildness of a land and the wanting of a woman and make them his own.

A town deep in the Rockies, 1861—where outlaws ruled the roost, and life came cheap.

1

Skye Fargo wasn't expecting trouble. He'd been riding for days to reach the town of Meridian, and once he was over a high pass he'd have only six or seven miles to go. It was midmorning when he reached the top of Bald Peak and the cleft that would take him from one side of the range to the other.

That high up, the air was cool, even in the summer. A hawk circled over the timber and a raven eyed him from a roost in a tree.

The pass was a cleft with high walls, wide enough for a wagon. It was like riding through a tunnel without a roof.

Out of habit, Fargo rode with his hand on his Colt.

This was wild country. The Shadow Mountains, as they were called, were the haunt of hostiles and outlaws. The unwary paid for being careless with their lives.

Fargo had lived too long on the raw edge to let his guard down. So it was that as he came to the end of the pass, he drew rein to scan the slopes below.

A big man, wide at the shoulders and narrow at the hips, Fargo wore buckskins and a white hat nearly brown from the dust of many miles. His eyes were as blue as a high-country lake. His face was flint-hard, and uncommonly pleasing to the female eye. One look at him and most folks realized he wasn't the sort of hombre you tangled with if you were in your right mind.

But someone decided to.

Fargo glimpsed a flash of light near a cluster of giant rock slabs. He'd seen similar flashes before—the gleam of sunlight off metal. Hunching forward, Fargo used his spurs. The Ovaro exploded into motion just as a shot cracked and a leaden bee buzzed his ear. Drawing the Colt, Fargo fired at the slabs even as he reined sharply to the right.

He needed to hunt cover. Except for scattered boulders, the ground was open to the tree line, making it easy to pick a rider off. Or so the bushwhacker no doubt hoped.

Bent low over his saddle horn, Fargo galloped hard. He worried the shooter would try to bring down the Ovaro. To prevent that he fired twice more to make the man hunt cover.

A large boulder loomed. It wasn't big enough to shield the Ovaro but Fargo put it between him and the rifleman to make it harder for the man to hit them.

His best hope was to reach a line of pines that came within a few hundred feet of the crest. He nearly got a cramp in his neck from looking over his shoulder for another flash of sunlight. Strangely, there wasn't any. There had just been that one shot.

Then Fargo saw why.

A man on a sorrel had broken from the cluster of slabs and was making for the forest.

Maybe his own shots had come too close for comfort, Fargo realized. Or it could be the killer figured to reach the woods first and cut him off.

Like hell, Fargo vowed. The Ovaro was second to no other horse when it came to speed and stamina. He'd pitted the stallion against the fine mounts of the Comanche and the Sioux and in races with whites, and the Ovaro nearly always proved their better.

Pebbles clattering from under the stallion's flying hooves, Fargo made it to the pines without being shot. Once in among them, he raced down the slope, flying for more than fifty yards before common sense warned him to haul on the reins and give a listen.

The mountain had gone quiet. The bushwhacker could be anywhere.

Quietly, quickly, Fargo replaced the spent cartridges in the Colt. He added a sixth since he normally left the chamber under the hammer empty.

Shadow dappled the woodland. For that matter, much of the range was darker than usual. It was why people called them the Shadow Mountains.

Fargo gigged the stallion. He was alert for movement of any kind. Once, a hint of motion made him raise the Colt but it was only a jay taking wing.

What spooked it? Fargo wondered. Reining behind a spruce, he climbed down. He twirled the Colt into his holster, shucked his Henry rifle from the saddle scabbard and worked the lever to feed a round into the chamber.

Tucked at the knees, Fargo worked around the spruce and over to a fir. He hunkered and studied the shadows near where the jay had been. Just when he was about convinced he must be mistaken, a head and a hat poked from behind a trunk and scoured the woods in his direction.

Fargo froze. The man had a fair idea where he was but didn't know for sure. He watched as the head swung from side to side and then disappeared. At that distance he couldn't tell much other than the man had a beard a lot bushier than his own.

Fargo waited. With any luck the killer would come to him. It depended on how much the man wanted him dead.

Apparently a lot, because it wasn't a minute later that Fargo spied a figure flitting from tree to tree.

Inwardly, Fargo smiled. Slowly raising the Henry, he pressed the stock to his shoulder, his cheek to the brass, and sighted down the barrel. All he needed was a clear shot.

The man didn't give it to him. Whoever he was, the

killer was always on the move and never showed more than a small part of himself.

Fargo decided to go for the chest. He saw the man dart behind an evergreen. Shifting slightly, he fixed his sights on the other side. Sure enough, the man reappeared. Fargo held his breath, and fired.

The Henry boomed and bucked and the figure plunged to the ground.

Fargo didn't go rushing down. He stalked through the vegetation until he spied a pair of legs jutting from behind a log. They were toes-up and weren't moving.

Suspicious of a trick, Fargo eased onto his belly and snaked to the log. Taking off his hat, he slowly raised his head high enough to see over.

The bushwhacker was flat on his back. Tall and lean, he had dark eyes wide in shock. His clothes were store bought and not in good condition, and his hat was pinned under his head and partially flattened. In the middle of his shirt was a spreading scarlet stain. His chest rose and fell in labored breaths, and each time he breathed out, scarlet bubbled. Pink froth rimmed his thin lips.

Jamming his own hat back on, Fargo stood and trained the Henry on his would-be killer. He stepped over the log, kicked the man's Spencer well out of reach, and snatched a Remington from a holster and tossed it after the rifle.

The man glared the whole while.

Stepping back, Fargo cradled the Henry. "What were you after? Money?"

The bushwhacker went on glaring.

"Stupid son of a bitch," Fargo said. "I've got barely ten dollars in my poke."

The man tried to speak but all that came out were puffs of breath. Gritting his blood-flecked teeth, he tried again, gasping, "Not . . . money."

"What then? My horse?" Fargo looked around. The killer's

sorrel was down the slope a ways, tied to a tree. "You've already got one."

"Not . . . horse," the man gasped.

"You tried to blow out my wick for the hell of it?" Fargo had met some who would. Human wolves with no more conscience than a rock.

"You," the bearded man said. "Kill . . . you."

Fargo's brow puckered in puzzlement. "You were waiting for *me*?"

A crafty gleam came into those beady eyes.

"Hold on," Fargo said, looking the man up and down. "I've never seen you before. Why in hell would you want to kill me?"

The man didn't answer.

Fargo was at a loss. No one knew he was coming to Meridian. Not even the person who sent for him, since he'd never answered her letter. "Who are you?"

The man glared.

"I'll make a deal," Fargo said. "Tell me what I want to know and I'll bury you. Don't, and I'll leave you for the coyotes and the buzzards." Some men wouldn't care one way or the other but he had nothing else to bargain with.

"Clemens," the man got out. "Handle . . . is Clemens."

"I'll ask you again. Why ambush me?"

"Stop . . . you," Clemens said.

"Stop me from what?" Fargo asked, and even as he did, it hit him. "To stop me from reaching town? From talking to her?"

"You do," Clemens gasped, "you die."

"Are you the reason she sent for me?"

Clemens snorted, or tried to. Crimson drops dribbled from his nose and more blood frothed his mouth. "Others will get you. *He'll* get you."

"Who?"

Closing his eyes, Clemens shuddered. His breathing

became shallow and his face paled before Fargo's eyes. The man wasn't long for this world.

Fargo went through his pockets. He found twenty-two dollars in coins and a few bills, a folding knife, and a pocket watch that didn't work. It told him nothing.

Fargo retrieved the sorrel. He untied it and brought it over and looped the reins around a broken branch on the log. Then he rummaged through the saddlebags. There were spare clothes, as worn as those Clemens had on, spare socks with holes in them, cartridges, some coffee and a coffeepot, a tin cup and a fork and a fire steel and flint for starting a fire.

Turning to his would-be assassin, Fargo squatted and poked him.

Clemens opened his eyes.

"Last chance to tell me who is behind this."

"Go . . . to . . . hell."

"I'll find out anyway," Fargo said. "I'm going on to Meridian." Odds were, whoever didn't want him there would make themselves known.

"Tried to . . . help . . . pard," Clemens managed to get out as more blood oozed.

"I still need a name."

Clemens didn't answer.

Standing, Fargo aimed his Colt at the center of Clemens's forehead. "Reckon I'll put you out of your misery, then."

For the first time fear showed in the other's eyes. "You said . . . you'd wait . . . and bury me."

"I said I'd bury you," Fargo agreed. "I never said I'd wait around for you to die."

"Bastard."

"Nice meeting you, too." Fargo stroked the trigger.

6

2

The town of Meridian wasn't much. A main street flanked by a dozen businesses and houses and cabins, several short side streets, and that was it.

There was the usual general store and millinery and a livery. A saloon quenched the thirst of those who craved hard liquor. A church at one end reminded the sinners that the Almighty was watching over them.

Meridian was small but it still had a marshal; a sign on a small building sandwiched between the general store and a butcher's proclaimed the fact.

Drawing rein at a hitch rail, Fargo dismounted. He was the focus of many a passerby. Or, rather, the body draped over the sorrel was. He tied off both animals and stepped to the door and walked on in.

Sprawled in a chair, his boots propped on his desk, the marshal was snoring loud enough to wake the dead. When Fargo smacked the desk, the lawman started and sat up so fast, he nearly spilled from his chair. "What in the world?" He had a belly that bulged over his belt and more than one chin.

"Having a nice nap?" Fargo asked.

The marshal colored. "Here now. Who are you and what's your business?"

"I brought you some business, Marshal—?"

"Cripdin," the lawman said. "Theodore Cripdin." He

adjusted his hat. "You shouldn't ought to scare folks like that."

"I was afraid if I poked you," Fargo said, "you might scream."

Cripdin scowled. "I'll thank you to show more respect. And I'll ask you again. Who are you and why are you bothering me?"

"Come out and see for yourself."

Reluctantly, the lawman heaved out of the chair. His belly quivering like a bowl of pudding, he came around and hitched at his holster. "This better be important. I'm a busy man."

"I can see that, Theodore," Fargo said.

"It's Marshal Cripdin to you."

Fargo opened the door and held it for him. "Most places I've been, bodies are important."

"Bodies?" Cripdin repeated. He stepped out and lurched to a stop. His mouth dropped and he shook his head as if he couldn't believe what he saw. "Good God. There *is* a body."

"He said his name was Clemens," Fargo told him. "He tried to kill me."

Marshal Cripdin went around the hitch rail, gripped the dead man by the hair, and raised his head for a look. "I'll be damned. Harve Clemens. You say he tried to kill you?"

Fargo nodded.

"Then how come you're still alive? He has a string of killings to his credit half as long as your arm."

"He was piss-poor at it," Fargo said.

"I don't buy that for a minute," Cripdin declared. He tilted his head. "Say, who are you, anyhow? And what are you doing in Meridian?"

Fargo gave his name. "The rest is my business."

"Like hell," Cripdin said. "You've been involved in a killing."

By now a crowd had gathered. Everyone was talking in hushed tones as if afraid they'd disturb the dead man.

8

"Blasingame won't like it one bit," a man said louder than the rest. "He's liable to ride in here with his gang and set them loose on us."

That caused quite a stir.

"Hold on there, folks," Marshal Cripdin said, raising his arms to get their attention. "It was an outsider who done in Clemens. We're not to blame."

"Thank God," a woman exclaimed.

All eyes turned to Fargo. None were friendly. An older man chomping tobacco stopped chewing to spit, wipe his mouth with his sleeve, and say, "Do you have any notion what you've done, you lunkhead?"

"We get in trouble because of this," a younger man said, "we'll hold you to account."

Fargo smiled and said, "Go to hell."

For all of ten seconds no one said a word. Then a woman hollered, "What did you just say?"

Fargo stepped to the body and gave it a hard smack on the back. "This son of a bitch tried to dry gulch me. There isn't one of you who wouldn't have done the same as I did."

That gave them pause. Whispers were exchanged, and furtive glances cast.

Marshal Cripdin cleared his throat. "Enough for now, folks. I'm fixing to question this man and will get to the bottom of things. Go on about your own affairs."

Grumbling and muttering, the people dispersed.

"As for you," the lawman said to Fargo, "go in my office and wait for me. I need to get this body off the street. I'll take him to the undertaker's and be back in ten minutes or so." He undid the sorrel's reins and plodded down the street with it in tow.

"Sure," Fargo said to himself. Climbing on the Ovaro, he reined the opposite way and was almost to the church when he spied the number he was looking for: 117 was a frame house bordered by a picket fence. He tied the stallion to a slat, opened the gate, and went up a footpath to the porch.

The polite thing to do was rap lightly. Fargo pounded, shaking the door nearly off its hinges.

Someone squealed that they were coming and for him to keep his britches on.

Fargo pounded again.

The door was jerked open and he was wreathed in perfume.

A young woman about twenty years old was framed in the doorway. Beautiful blond hair crowned an oval face with lively green eyes, full cheeks, and ripe lips. Her dress had a bow at the throat, and she was wearing an apron. Looking him up and down, she said softly, "Oh my."

Fargo felt a familiar tingle, low down. Doffing his hat, he smiled. "Howdy, ma'am. Would you be Mrs. Hemmings? Glenda Hemmings?"

"Goodness, no," the young woman said. "I'm Miss Hemmings. Mrs. Hemmings is my mother."

Fargo introduced himself, adding, "I believe I'm expected. She sent for me."

"Yes, I know." Rather sheepishly, the young woman moved aside so he could enter. "I'm Jennifer, by the way."

Fargo liked how she filled out her dress. And those lips; he imagined sucking on them while she squirmed under him.

"Are you all right?" Jennifer asked. "A strange look just came over you."

"Fine, ma'am," Fargo said.

The inside of the house was as well kept as the outside. A tantalizing scent filled the hallway, and he sniffed and asked, "What's that smell?"

"We're baking," Jennifer said. "Come. I'll take you to Mother."

The kitchen was warm and cozy. Not one but two women were busy; another young one was at a table, kneading dough. An older woman, who couldn't be much more than forty, had just opened a stove and was inspecting a tray of cookies. She heard his spurs jingle and glanced over.

"Who's this?"

"Mr. Fargo," Jennifer said. "The man you sent for."

Glenda Hemmings straightened. She was every bit as good-looking as her daughters, only her hair was brown and her bosom more ample. Appearing nervous, she wiped her hands on her apron and came over and offered one. "How do you do. I must say, this is a surprise. I never heard back so I assumed you weren't coming."

"After what you did," Fargo said, shaking, "how could I not?"

The young woman at the table asked, "What does he mean by that, Mother?" She was a lot like her sister only a year or so younger and her hair was a sandy color and hung past her shoulders to the small of her back.

"Never you mind, Constance," Glenda said. She coughed and pulled out a chair. "Where are my manners? Have a seat, Mr. Fargo. Would you like anything? Lemonade, per-haps? Or tea? Or how about some coffee?"

"I'd kill for some coffee," Fargo said. He'd had only a single cup that morning. Usually he downed three or four but he was running low.

"It would be my pleasure. I happen to have some on the stove." Glenda bustled about taking a cup and saucer from a cupboard and filling the cup and setting it in front of him.

Jennifer and Constance stood by the table, apparently fascinated.

"Would you care for sugar and cream?" Glenda asked.

Ordinarily Fargo had his black but he decided to treat himself. "Don't mind if I do." He admired how her dress clung to her thighs as she moved, and how her bosom swelled when she bent over.

"Anything else?"

Fargo sipped, and smiled. She made good coffee. He

shook his head, saying, "We'd better get to it. I've come a long ways."

"Certainly." Glenda faced her girls. "You two go to your rooms. Mr. Fargo and I have something to discuss."

"But Mother," Jennifer said.

"We can't stay?" Constance asked.

"No, you can't," Glenda said, moving behind them and shooing them along. "It's adult talk."

"We're adults," Jennifer said.

"You only think you are but you have a lot to learn yet," Glenda said. "Now go."

The pair dutifully obeyed but they weren't happy about it.

Jennifer grinned mischievously over her shoulder at Fargo and gave a little wave.

"They're good girls," Glenda said. "After all they've been through, I'm proud they've held up so well."

Reaching into a pocket, Fargo pulled out the letter she'd sent. "This caught up with me at Fort Leavenworth."

"I sent it over six months ago," Glenda said. "After all this time, I didn't think you were coming."

Fargo unfolded the sheet of paper and read the pertinent part aloud. "I need your help. They say you're the best tracker alive, and I'd like you to track down my husband. It won't be easy. He's a wanted outlaw. And he has a pack of killers who ride with him. But if you do it, in return I'm offering you half the bounty."

"Is that what brought you? The money?"

"No," Fargo said. He slid his fingers into the envelope and carefully held the half-dozen small brown strands in his palm. "These did. Are they what I think they are?"

"Yes," Glenda said softly. "They're my"—she paused and glanced down at herself and blushed—"love hairs."

3

Fargo had heard them called a lot of things but never that. "I'll be damned," he said, and puffed on those in his palm. They flew off, swirling and turning, and landed on the table.

"Please don't," Glenda said. "We eat off of there." She took the bottom of her apron and swept the hairs to the floor.

"I have to hand it to you, lady," Fargo said. "When I unwrapped them and realized what they were, I laughed so damn hard my sides hurt."

"You thought it was funny?"

"I think it's smart as hell," Fargo said.

"Good. I was hoping it would get your attention. They say that you're a—how shall I put this?—notorious womanizer."

"And you reckoned your puss hairs would perk my interest?"

"I'm desperate," Glenda said. "I wanted to get your attention."

"You did a damn fine job."

"I'll make it worth your while."

Fargo stared at the junction of her thighs. "I'm counting on that."

Glenda blushed. Pulling out the chair across from him, she sat. "Right now there's something more important to discuss. The man I want you to track down."

"I'm not a bounty hunter," Fargo enlightened her. "I'm a scout."

"I know," Glenda said. "People say you can track as good as an Apache. And that's what it will take. You're my last hope of finding him."

Fargo swallowed some coffee. "Your husband, the letter said."

"Yes. You see, Hemmings isn't my real name. I took it to hide who I am." Glenda wrung her hands and bit her lip. "My real name is Glenda Blasingame."

Fargo remembered hearing the name out in the street. "The hombre who has everyone so scared?"

"The very same," Glenda said. "He left me a few years ago. We were living in Saint Louis at the time, and one day he up and announced he was leaving me and heading west. The next I heard, he'd turned outlaw. They call him the terror of the Shadow Mountains. He's robbed stages, held up the Meridian bank, and worse. The stage company has put five thousand dollars on his head, dead or alive. The bank has done the same. That's ten thousand in bounty money, and like I said, I'm willing to split it with you."

"Generous," Fargo said.

"I know what you're thinking. That you'd have to do all the work. That you'd be out there risking your life while I sit here safe and sound. Am I right?"

"Something like that," Fargo admitted.

"But that's just it," Glenda said. "I won't be sitting here. You'll take me with you." She smiled. "I'm the bait that will lure my husband in."

About to take another swallow, Fargo said, "You weren't joshing when you said you were desperate."

"It's the only thing that might work. Others have tried to hunt Cord down and failed. That's his full name, by the way. Cord Blasingame."

"Some handle," Fargo said.

"And some man. He's as handsome as you, and as tricky as they come."

Her tone prompted Fargo to remark, "You still care for him, sounds like."

"I'd be lying if I said I didn't. Even though he left me, I still have strong feelings."

"But not so strong you wouldn't turn him in for the bounty."

Glenda fussed with her hair. "You must think I'm terrible. But the truth is, he took all our money when he walked out. It wasn't much. But it left me penniless with two daughters to take care of."

"They're grown enough to find work."

"They had jobs in Saint Louis, yes," Glenda said. "But seamstress work and cooking don't earn much. We've barely been scraping by. I'm tired of it. Call me selfish if you must but I want better for them, and for me. Can you blame me?"

"It's not for me to say."

"Some would," Glenda said bitterly. "They'd accuse me of betraying my own husband. Call me a Judas." She bowed her head and said softly, "Life is so unfair."

Fargo had been mulling her offer. "Let's say I agree to go after him. I don't much like the notion of you being bait."

"Why not? If he hears I'm with you, he's bound to come. Well, the girls and me."

"Them too?"

"As you pointed out, they're full grown. They can ride, and they're half-fair rifle shots."

"No," Fargo said. He had a hunch it would take a while to track this Blasingame down, and the Shadow Mountains were no place for amateurs.

"Don't you see? If we have the girls along, Cord won't suspect a thing. He knows I'd never put them in peril. He'll

15

likely figure you're our guide and come riding right into our camp."

"I'm still against it."

Glenda sat back. "You're being unreasonable. All I ask is that you think it over. You're welcome to stay the night and give me your decision in the morning. If that's all right."

Fargo almost laughed. Mind spending a night in a house with three beauties? "Fine by me."

"Good." Glenda nodded, pleased. "Now then. Would you care for something to eat? Or perhaps you'd like to rest up after your long ride?"

"What I'd like," Fargo said, "is to visit a whiskey mill."

"Oh." Glenda sounded disappointed.

Draining his cup, Fargo set it down. "I'll tend to my horse later."

"We'll be here."

Fargo had a stop to make before the saloon. He didn't bother knocking.

Marshal Theodore Cripdin was at his desk, scribbling. Without looking up he said, "I'll be with you in a minute."

Leaning against the wall, Fargo folded his arms. "No hurry."

The lawman glanced up. "You!" he blurted. "I told you to come here and wait for me."

"What can you tell me about Cord Blasingame?"

Cripdin set down the pencil and leaned back, his belly shaking with every movement. "You're commencing to annoy me, mister. When I give an order I expect it to be obeyed."

"Blasingame," Fargo said.

The lawman scowled and muttered something, then said, "What do you want to know? He's the scourge of the territory. He showed up here two, maybe three years ago, and before long had a gang under him. They're the deadliest long riders on two legs, and that's no lie."

"Why haven't you arrested him?"

"You think I haven't tried? I've gone out after him more times than I care to admit and I always come back empty-handed. He's too smart for me. And he knows the mountains better than anybody."

It was rare for a man to admit his shortcomings; Fargo's estimation of the lawman rose a notch. "How many in this gang of his?"

"Eight," Cripdin said. "No, seven, seeing as how you killed Clemens."

"And if a man wanted to find them, where would he look?"

"Are you loco?"

Fargo waited.

"It's the bounty, isn't it?" Cripdin sighed. "Mister, you're not the only one who thought he'd get rich by killing Cord Blasingame. By my count half a dozen men have gone after him and not one came back."

"You don't know for sure he killed them."

"True. It could have been the other outlaws. Word has it they're protective of him. But the who isn't important. All that matters is the other bounty men never came back." The marshal scratched his belly. "As to where to find the outlaws, your guess is as good as mine. Folks claim they have a hideout deep in the mountains."

"I'm obliged." Fargo turned to go.

"Hold on. I still need to hear about Clemens."

"I shot him. He died." Fargo opened the door and walked out. He wasn't halfway to the saloon when ponderous steps matched his own.

"Damn it, man. You can't ignore me. I'm the law."

"You're something," Fargo said.

Cripdin grabbed his arm. "Now see here. I've put up with all I'm going to. I want you to come back so I can make out a report."

Fargo pulled loose. "Make it without me."

The lawman started to raise his hand to his revolver.

"You don't want to do that."

"Why not?"

Just like that, Fargo's Colt was in his hand. He spun it forward and he spun it backward and flipped it and caught it and twirled it into his holster, all so fast, the lawman's jaw fell.

"God Almighty."

Fargo kept on toward the saloon.

"Listen, mister. I don't know why you have it in for me. I've got a job to do, is all. When can I expect you to stop by?"

Fargo stopped and looked at him. "About an hour should do."

"I'll be waiting."

Fargo pushed on the batwings.

The Ace's High was a rarity; it boasted a mahogany bar, a small chandelier, and a painting of a near-naked woman lounging on cushions. Although it was early yet, more than a dozen locals were drinking and playing cards.

Fargo smacked the bar and asked for a bottle of Monongahela. It wasn't until he drained his first glass at a gulp that he felt more like his usual self. He hadn't let on to Glenda Blasingame but he was mad as hell. That bushwhacking at the pass—somehow, the outlaws had learned he was coming. And only three people, besides him, knew.

An empty chair at a corner table beckoned. Fargo claimed it, refilled his glass, and swirled the whiskey. A few more and he would go back and confront Glenda over how she nearly got him killed.

"Buy a girl a drink?"

Fargo looked up. He'd noticed a dove over at the end of the bar but hadn't paid much attention to her. Now that he did, he liked what he saw. Black hair, ruby lips, and melons that threatened to burst her dress at the seams. "What do we have here?"

"What do you think?" Smirking, she placed her left foot on an empty chair and slowly slid her dress up until the hem was above her knee. She touched a finger to her inner thigh and enticingly ran it up under her dress. "Like what you see?"

4

It had been almost two weeks since Fargo was with a woman. For a man like him, who liked cards, whiskey and females more than just about anything, that was a long time to go without. "What do they call you?"

"Tassy." She playfully swung her leg from side to side, and grinned. "How about you buy me a drink, and then who knows?"

"Fetch a glass and join me."

Tassy scooted to the bar and was back in two shakes of a lamb's tail. She pulled a chair next to his and sat so their arms brushed. "To the brim, if you please."

Fargo filled her glass.

She watched him intently. "My, oh my, you are easy on the eyes. Has anyone ever told you that?"

"No," Fargo lied.

"The moment I set eyes on you, I wanted you to give me a poke."

"I bet you say that to everyone with a pecker," Fargo said.

Tassy squealed with mirth. "You just come right out with it, don't you?"

Fargo thought of something. "How long have you been working here?"

"At the Ace's High? Going on about four years now. I drifted in one day and liked it and stayed." Tassy sipped and happily sighed. "It's not as hectic as in the big cities.

Why, in Kansas City a girl is on her back twelve hours of the day. Here, I get to pick and choose." She winked. "And I choose you."

"What can you tell me about Cord Blasingame?"

About to take another sip, Tassy paused. "Why do you want to know about him?"

"One of his men tried to kill me."

"Oh God," Tassy said, and set the glass down. "You're the one everyone is talking about. The one who brought Clemens in."

"You knew him?"

Tassy shrugged. "All the gang drift into town from time to time. Well, except the breed. Clemens stopped for a drink now and then."

"Cripdin didn't arrest him?"

Tassy snorted. "As a tin star he's next to worthless. Blasingame himself could stroll down Main Street and Cripdin would hide in his office, quaking in his boots."

"A yellow lawman?" Most badge-toters Fargo knew were as tough as rawhide.

"Let's just say he's not the bravest and let it go at that."

"Why do the people let him stay in office?"

"He's the only one who wants the job. The last election, no one ran against him."

"Must make it easy for Blasingame," Fargo remarked.

"Now there's another handsome devil. He's just as good-looking as you." Tassy put her hand on his. "I should warn you, mister. His gang won't take kindly to you killing Clemens. Could be they'll come gunning for you."

"Let them," Fargo said, thinking that it would make his hunt easier.

"You don't know what you're saying," Tassy said. "They're killers, every one. There's Mills, who likes to use a bowie. Hardy, who carries a sawed-off shotgun. And the breed. God, be careful of the breed."

Fargo ticked them off in his head. The marshal had told him there were seven. "What about the other four? Do you know their names?"

She didn't even have to think about it. "Zeke, Davies, Nesbit and Billy Barnes."

"How many of them have you had under the sheets?"

Tassy blinked, and laughed a high, nervous laugh. "Just one. But don't ask me which. I'm not the kind to be poked and tell."

"They do their drinking in here?"

"Sometimes, sure."

"And no one does anything about it?"

"What could we? We're peaceable folks, not gun hands."

"This is some town," Fargo said.

"Why do you say that?"

Instead of answering Fargo took a swig from the bottle. "Since you know so much, where do they hang their gun belts?"

Tassy uttered that high, nervous laugh again. "How in the world would I know that? They're outlaws. They never tell anyone where they hide out."

"If you say so."

"Can we stop talking about them now? I'd rather talk about you, and how good-looking you are."

"How much for a poke?"

Tassy smiled and traced a circle on the back of his hand with her fingernail. "Usually it's five dollars but for you it'll be free."

"Why so generous?"

"Because as I keep telling you, you're handsome as hell. And I like handsome men as much as I like peaches and cream."

"Do tell," Fargo said. She didn't seem to realize the mistake she'd just made.

Tassy leaned against him and huskily asked, "So is it yes or is it no?"

"How about I finish the bottle and make up my mind?" Fargo said.

She sat back. "I don't see why you have to think about it. I'm not that hard on the eyes my own self."

"No," Fargo agreed, "you're not."

That seemed to mollify her. She traced another circle on his hand and rimmed her lips with the tip of her tongue. "I'll make it worth your while."

"That shouldn't be hard since it's free."

The corners of Tassy's mouth curled down. "I can't tell if you're teasing or insulting me."

"I never insult a lady."

"Good." Tassy grinned and wriggled her bottom. "So why are you in Meridian, anyhow? Just passing through?"

Fargo decided to be truthful. Her reaction would tell him a lot. "I'm going to kill Cord Blasingame."

It was as if someone had stabbed her. She stiffened and paled. "What did he ever do to you?"

"He tried to have me killed," Fargo said. "He sent Clemens to the pass to stop me from getting here."

"Maybe not," Tassy said. "Clemens could have been there on his own."

"It's too much of a coincidence."

"No. Hear me out." Tassy fiddled with a button on her dress. "They don't always do everything together. They scatter sometimes and range all over. Two or three might hold someone up while others are off stealing cattle. That time they robbed the bank, only five of them took part."

"You know an awful lot about how they operate."

"Everyone does," Tassy said. "It's not as if they keep it a secret. People coming over the pass have been robbed before. Clemens might not have known you from Adam. Maybe he just wanted your poke."

Fargo remembered the outlaw gasping that he was there to stop him from reaching town. So much for her idea. But he kept it to himself for the time being.

"It could be Cord Blasingame had nothing to do with it," Tassy was saying.

"If you say so."

Tassy brightened. "So you've changed your mind? You're not going after him?"

"No," Fargo said. "I still am." He figured to let it go at that but she had other ideas.

"What possible reason can you have for wanting to take his life?"

"There's the bounty."

"Oh. You're one of those." Tassy's eyes flashed with anger. "I'll never understand hunting someone down for money."

"You sell your body for money."

Tassy pushed back her chair, balled her fists, and stood. "I've changed my mind. You don't get to poke me. Not now or ever."

"They're your tits," Fargo said.

"Damn right they are. And I don't have to let anyone touch them I don't want to." Turning, she walked off in a huff, pushing a man who got in her way. At the batwings she paused to glare at him, and pushed on out.

"Well, now," Fargo said. Meridian was turning out to be a damned interesting town. He refilled his glass, intending to sit there a while and relax.

It wasn't two minutes later that the batwings creaked again and in came Marshal Theodore Cripdin. He wasn't there for a drink. He spied Fargo and came straight for the corner table.

"I just had a few words with Tassy McCullen."

"You ask her for a poke?"

"What? No. But I want to ask you to forget about going after Cord Blasingame."

"That's your business how?"

"I'm the law," Cripdin reminded him yet again. "It's my job to bring him in."

24

"The bank and the stage company think different," Fargo said.

"Them and their damn bounties. It ought to be illegal to put a price on a man's head. A man shouldn't be hunted like a deer or a bear."

"Blasingame is an outlaw."

"So? He's entitled to a trial, the same as everybody else. But he'll never get one with this 'dead or alive' business."

"All he has to do is turn himself in and no one can collect it."

"Oh, sure. And be put on trial and hung. What kind of jackass do you take him for?"

"No one forced him to become an outlaw."

"Judge, jury and executioner, is that it? It could be something drove him to it. It could be there's more to him than you think."

"There has to be," Fargo said, "when whores and lawmen take his side."

"You have me all wrong," Cripdin said. "I'm just doing my job." He appeared about to say more but just then a gray-haired man in clothes that had seen a lot of use and a broad-brimmed brown hat entered the saloon. A Smith & Wesson was in a holster on his left side, worn butt-forward for a cross draw.

Cripdin's Adam's apple bobbed and he started to turn. "I've said my piece. I hope you come to your senses." He lumbered out.

At last Fargo could drink in peace. Or so he thought until the gray-haired man came over.

"You're the one I'm looking for."

"This isn't my day," Fargo said.

"I hear tell you're after the bounty money on Cord Blasingame."

"Word spreads fast."

"That it does," the man said. "My handle is Zeke Bell. I ride with him. I figure to stop you by killing you myself."

5

Fargo was caught off guard. His glass was in his right hand, halfway to his mouth. His Colt was in his holster, partway under the table.

Zeke's gun hand was inches from his Smith & Wesson, his thumb hooked in his gun belt. "Any last words?" he said.

"Just like this?" Fargo said.

"Just like this," Zeke said. "I don't back-shoot. I go after someone, I go at them straight up."

"An outlaw with scruples," Fargo said. He was stalling while he inched his arm lower.

"I have a few," Zeke said. "It comes from being older than Methuselah."

The man didn't look that old to Fargo. The gray was premature. "Do I get to finish my drink?"

"Be my guest," Zeke said. "As soon as you set the glass down, we'll get to it."

"What if I don't set it down?" Fargo said, and threw the glass at the outlaw's face.

Zeke tried to duck but some of the whiskey caught him in the eyes. Backpedaling, blinking furiously, he clawed for the Smith & Wesson.

Fargo heaved out of his chair. He drew as his holster cleared the table and fanned a shot that punched Zeke in the gut. Doubled over, Zeke brought up the Smith & Wesson. Fargo fanned a second shot that knocked Zeke back a step, fanned a third that punched Zeke in the chest, fanned a final shot that cored Zeke Bell's forehead and burst out the back of his cranium.

Zeke tottered, dead on his feet. His mouth worked and his knees gave and he crashed to the floor.

The saloon was deathly still. Mouths hung open, eyes were wide. The bartender forgot himself and filled a glass to overflowing.

Fargo reloaded while walking around the table. Squatting, he went through the man's pockets.

"Should you be doing that?" someone said.

Fargo helped himself to a poke. He didn't count the money; he'd do that later. A comb and some snuff he left alone.

Outside, someone hollered and boots pounded. Back into the saloon rushed Marshal Cripdin, who stopped short at the sight of the blood and brains on the floor.

"God in heaven."

Fargo righted his chair, sat back down, and poured. He ignored the whisperings and the stares. People were looking in the window and over the batwings.

Careful not to step anywhere near the blood, the lawman came over. "Did you have to do it?"

"He came here to kill me," Fargo said. "Thanks for arresting him, by the way."

"I had no idea he was Zeke Bell."

Fargo stared at him.

"What?"

"This is some town," Fargo said again. "It seems Bell heard I'm after Blasingame and reckoned on stopping me."

"I wonder how he found out."

"The whole damn town must know by now," Fargo said. "I'm more interested in how outlaws can come into Meridian and not be thrown behind bars."

"I don't like what you're suggesting."

"And I don't give a good damn what you don't like."

27

Fargo rose and leaned on the table. "How much do they pay you to look the other way? Or is that your yellow streak is as wide as your back?"

"I won't be talked to like this."

"But you'll let a killer come gunning for me. You walked right by him when he came in." Stepping around the table, Fargo punched the lawman in the gut.

Cripdin folded in half and had to clutch a chair to keep from falling. "You can't . . ." he got out, "hit a lawman."

"Watch me," Fargo said, and drawing his Colt, he slammed the barrel against Cripdin's temple. The marshal sprawled on the floor, quivering like a dumpling.

Statues filled the saloon and were frozen at the window.

Twirling the Colt into his holster, Fargo placed his hands on his hips. "Spread the word," he said. "I'm through being played with. Fight shy of me, or else."

"See here," a man found his voice. "You can't threaten the whole town."

"I just did," Fargo said. "From here on out, anyone gets in my way, there'll be hell to pay. You've been warned." Grabbing his bottle, he stepped over the marshal and walked out. No one tried to stop him. In fact, they scattered from his path like sheep from a wolf.

Fargo went up the middle of the street. Townspeople watched from doors and windows. He'd created quite a stir, which was exactly what he wanted. Word was bound to reach Cord Blasingame that he'd bucked out two of Blasingame's men. With any luck, Blasingame would come after him and he could get this over with.

The Ovaro was dozing. Fargo untied the reins and led it to the back of the house. He stripped the saddle and saddle blanket and bridle and hung them over the fence. Taking a picket pin and a small coil of rope from his saddlebags, he used a rock to pound the pin into the ground.

The saddlebags over his shoulder, the Henry in his left hand, he started for the back door.

Jennifer and Constance were on the back porch, waiting.

"Why use a pin?" the former asked. "The fence will keep your horse in."

"In case someone gets the wrong idea," Fargo said.

"Who would want to steal him?" Constance asked. "We're in the middle of town."

"Some town," Fargo said. He reached the steps and asked, "Which one of you wants to show me to my room?"

"We both will," Jennifer said.

Giggling and grinning, each of them took an arm and steered him through the back door and across the kitchen.

"Where's your mother?" Fargo asked as they brought him down the hall.

"She went shopping," Jennifer said. She was brazenly running her eyes up and down his body.

"We didn't expect you back so soon," Constance remarked.

"When our father used to go off drinking, he'd be out most of the night," Jennifer said.

"He do that a lot?"

"A lot more than Mother liked," Constance said. "She claimed he did it to get away from her."

"Did he?"

"Well, she did tend to nag a little," Jennifer said.

"More than a little," Constance said.

They guided Fargo up a flight of stairs and along a carpeted hall to a room at the end.

"This is the guest bedroom, Mother calls it. It's all yours."

"Anything you need, you only have to ask," Jennifer said. "Mother says we're to bend over backward to make your stay pleasant." She grinned and winked. "Not that I'd object to you bending me any way you please."

"Jen!" Constance exclaimed.

"Well, I wouldn't." Jennifer leaned toward Fargo. "Please don't mention that to our mother. She'd take a switch to us."

"At your age?" Fargo said.

"That doesn't mean no never mind to her," Constance said.

"Sometimes I think she likes to hit us," Jennifer said.

"She can be vicious," Constance mentioned.

"So she nags and she beats you. Is that why your father left her?"

Both girls let go of him and stepped back.

"There's more to it but we don't care to talk about it," Constance said.

"We like him, no matter what our mother says," Jennifer mentioned. "As fathers go, he's hardly the worst."

"He's an outlaw."

"So?"

Constance said sadly, "It's too bad there's so much bounty on his head. I don't want anything to happen to him."

"Me either," Jennifer said.

Fargo entered the bedroom. It was furnished with a bed, a chest of drawers, and a small table. A pitcher of water and a china basin had been set out. So had a neatly folded washcloth and towel. Lavender curtains covered the window.

"Here you go," Jennifer said, patting the bed. "You should be plenty comfortable." She smirked and gave him another wink.

"I worry about Father so much." Constance wouldn't let it drop. "Frankly, I wish we'd never come here. It was easier when there was distance between us."

"Forget about him for now," Jennifer said.

"I can't."

Fargo dropped his saddlebags and the Henry on the bed. "I take it neither of you are happy I'm here?"

"Sorry," Constance said, "but no."

Jennifer shrugged. "I don't want him hurt. But you're not the first to try to collect the bounty and I doubt you'll be the last."

"Thanks for the confidence."

"You don't realize what you're up against."

"I'm getting an idea," Fargo said.

"If you're smart you'll go," Constance said. "Pick up those saddlebags and saddle your horse and ride away while you can."

"I don't believe I will," Fargo said.

Constance frowned. "He's my father."

"Mine too," Jennifer said.

"It's nothing personal," Fargo told them.

"It is to me," Constance said, and her eyes suddenly brimmed with tears. "I don't care what he's done. I love him, damn you."

"Connie," Jennifer said softly.

"I hate this," Constance said. "I hate that Mother sent for him. I hate her, too."

"Connie, don't," Jennifer said, putting a hand on her arm.

A door slammed downstairs.

"Mother's home!" Jennifer exclaimed. "We better go." She steered her sister out, saying, "And you'd better mop those eyes. She sees you've been crying, she'll be mad."

Fargo took off his hat and buckskin shirt and gun belt, and filled the basin with water. He washed and dried, then opened his saddlebags and took out his razor and trimmed his beard. He didn't use pomade in his hair like some men did. A few strokes of his brush sufficed. He put on his spare shirt, strapped the Colt around his waist, and jammed his hat back on.

There was a light rap on the door.

"I'm decent," Fargo said.

Glenda came in. "Supper will be in an hour."

The thought of food made Fargo's stomach rumble. "Good to hear."

"Word is all over town that you killed another of Cord's men."

"Zeke Bell was his name."

"I know." Glenda beamed. "I was right to send for you. You'll finally do to my husband what all those others couldn't." She paused. "If he and his bunch don't kill you first, of course."

6

The dishes set out on the kitchen table made Fargo's mouth water. He hadn't had a home-cooked meal in months, and Glenda had gone to extra effort to please him.

There was vegetable soup to start things off. A heaping plate of roast beef, potatoes with asparagus, chopped carrots and hot rolls smeared in butter were the main course. For dessert they'd baked a cherry pie.

Fargo washed it down with four cups of piping hot coffee. When he was done he sat back and patted his belly and grinned. "Now I know why married men pack on so much weight."

"Cord never did," Glenda said. "He ate as much as you but he never put on an ounce. He took pride in being as hard as nails."

Fargo imagined her without her dress, and him as hard as a nail, and grinned.

"Would you care for more pie, Mr. Fargo?" Jennifer asked.

"No, thanks," Fargo said. The sisters had been subdued the whole meal. No doubt they were still upset about him going after their father, and he couldn't blame them.

"Now then," Glenda said, pushing her plate away. "Suppose we get to it. I'd very much like to hear how you plan to go about finding my husband."

"I'll take it as it comes," Fargo said.

Glenda waited, and when he didn't elaborate, she said, "That's it? It doesn't tell me anything."

"There's nothing else to tell."

Her lips pinched and she tapped a finger on the table. "You disappoint me. I expected better."

"Better how?"

"I don't know. You're the scout. The one they say can track down anyone or anything anywhere at anytime. But it sounds to me as if all you're going to do is twiddle your thumbs."

"I'll rest up tomorrow and the next day I'll start asking around," Fargo said to mollify her.

"You're going to waste an entire day doing nothing? What are you thinking?"

"Of my horse," Fargo said. "I rode hard to get here. It needs a day to rest up."

"You could rent another from the livery."

"No," Fargo said. He hardly ever used another horse. The Ovaro had saved his bacon more times than he could count and was the only mount he'd trust with his life.

"If you have to wait a day, so be it," Glenda said, not sounding happy at the prospect.

Constance cleared her throat. "We could show him around Meridian, Mother. Give him a feel for the town."

Fargo knew what he'd like to feel, and it wasn't buildings and hitch rails.

"That's hardly necessary," Glenda snapped. To Fargo she said, "Why don't you repair to the parlor? We'll clean up and join you directly."

Fargo shrugged. It was fine by him. He strolled down the hall and settled onto a settee. His full stomach and the peace and quiet, save for a few sounds from the kitchen, filled him with drowsiness. His eyelids grew leaden and it was all he could do to stay awake.

The women took so long that his chin started to dip to

his chest. He jerked his head up but his weary body wouldn't be denied. His chin bobbed again and he drifted off.

A warm hand on his shoulder woke him.

"Having a nice nap?" Jennifer asked.

Fargo yawned and stretched and accepted a cup of coffee she'd brought. She sat in a rocking chair as her mother and sister came around the corner, Constance bearing a tray of cookies.

"Sorry we took so long," Glenda said. "There were a lot of dishes and pots and pans to wash."

Fargo accepted a cookie and nibbled at it and reflected that if this was married life, it was boring as hell.

"I apologize for my manner earlier," Glenda said. "It's just that I want Cord brought to bay. The sooner he is, the sooner the killings and robberies stop." She folded her hands in her lap. "They prey on me so."

"You're not to blame," Fargo said.

"I know. But I feel as if I am. I was his wife, after all. Perhaps if I'd been a better one, he wouldn't have left me and the poor people he and his horrid men have murdered would still be alive."

"You're too hard on yourself, Mother," Constance said.

"He ran out on us, too," Jennifer said, "and you don't hear us apologizing for him."

In the hallway a man said, "Ain't you ladies somethin'?" and laughed.

A cookie in one hand, a cup of coffee in the other, Fargo looked over and turned to stone.

The man was short and squat and as filthy as a barnyard hog. His hat, his clothes, his skin, hadn't seen water in years, if ever. But it wasn't his filthiness that turned Fargo's blood to ice; it was the Sharps rifle he held level at his waist, the hammer cocked.

"You!" Glenda gasped.

"How do you do, missus," the man said. "I'm flattered

35

you remember me." He grinned at Jennifer and Constance. "And how are you girls these days? You remember me, don't you? Uncle Billy?"

"You're no relation of ours," Glenda practically hissed. "You were my husband's friend, is all. And what he saw in you is beyond me." She glared. "What are you doing here, Barnes?"

Fargo recollected that Billy Barnes was one of the names Tassy mentioned.

"I came into town with Zeke earlier," Barnes said, "and he went and got himself shot by this bastard." He wagged his Sharps at Fargo. "You have about five minutes left to live, mister."

"How dare you," Glenda said, rising. "You sneak into my home and threaten my guest."

Barnes laughed, showing gaps where teeth had been. "I didn't do no sneakin', bitch. The front door wasn't bolted."

"Bitch?" Livid with fury, Glenda moved toward him.

"No, you don't," Barnes said, training the Sharps on her. "I know Cord gave orders you're not to be harmed but he'll understand how it was when I tell him about Clemens and Zeke and you cozyin' with Zeke's killer."

"Cord doesn't want me hurt?"

"God knows why, but he's still got feelin's for you," Barnes said. "But enough about him." He focused on Fargo. "How is it that this hombre is sittin' in your parlor? And had supper with you? Don't deny it, neither, because I was spyin' through the kitchen window."

"You despicable wretch."

"Me?" Barnes said angrily. "You brought this feller to town, didn't you?"

Glenda balled her fists but didn't say anything.

"Cat got your tongue?" Barnes sneered. "Then let me spell it out for you. Zeke decided to brace the jasper who everyone says shot Clemens. Only he went and gots himself killed. And when I follow his killer, where does he go?

Straight to your house. He sups with you and here he sits as pretty as you please, makin' small talk with you and your gals."

"Are you through?"

"I'm just gettin' started." Barnes curled his finger around the trigger. "It's plain as can be that you and him are in cahoots."

Fargo stayed silent. The longer they argued, the better his chance of turning the tables. He went to lower the cup but Barnes instantly pointed the Sharps at him.

"I wouldn't, mister. You're dead but I can make it quick or I can shoot you to pieces." Barnes showed the gaps in his mouth again. "Own up to bein' her hired gun and it'll be smack between the eyes."

"I'm a scout, not a gun hand," Fargo said. Although folks did say he was uncommonly skilled with a six-shooter, as he'd demonstrated at the saloon.

"Scout?" Barnes said. "She hired you to hunt us down?"

"He's passing through and I put him up for the night," Glenda said. "That's all."

"And I'm the queen of England. You've stepped over the line, woman. Cord won't care anymore once he hears about this."

Neither of the girls had uttered a word but now Jennifer glanced at Fargo and then said, "Uncle Billy?"

"What, girl?" Barnes said without taking his eyes off Fargo.

"I remember you now," Jennifer said. "You used to come visit when I was little, before my father ever headed west."

"That was me," Barnes said, again without looking at her. "In fact, girl, I was the one who talked him into it for his own good."

"I remember how you bounced me on your knee," Jennifer said.

"Many a time," Barnes said.

37

"And stuck your hand up my dress."

Both Billy Barnes and Glenda turned sharply toward her and both said, "What?" at the same instant.

It was all the distraction Fargo needed. Heaving up off the settee, he let go of the cup and the cookie and launched himself at Barnes. The outlaw caught the movement out of the corner of his eye and tried to turn. Fargo rammed into him just as the Sharps went off, the heavy-caliber rifle booming like a cannon. He thought he heard the slug strike the wall near where he had been sitting, and then he and Barnes were on the floor and he jammed a knee to the outlaw's chest to pin him. He grabbed hold of the Sharps to wrest it loose, only to find that Billy Barnes was a lot stronger than he seemed and mad as a riled grizzly.

With a roar of rage, Barnes drove his fist into Fargo's gut. It felt like Fargo's stomach tried to burst out his spine. All his breath left him, and he sagged, momentarily weakened.

Barnes bucked and threw him off. Landing on his side, Fargo sought to get his hands under him. Barnes was on him in a heartbeat. A boot caught him in the ribs. The Sharps's stock arced at his head. He ducked, barely, and lost his hat. Still on his side, he drove his boot into Barnes's knee.

At the *crack*, Barnes howled. Where most men would have collapsed in agony, he attacked. His fist connected with Fargo's temple and Fargo almost blacked out. For a few seconds the parlor swam.

Desperate, Fargo shook his head to clear it and scrambled onto his hands and knees. His vision cleared just as an iron hand clamped on his throat.

A derringer muzzle was inches from his face. Above it, Barnes leered in triumph. "I have you now, you son of a bitch. I told you I'd blow out your wick for what you did to my pard and I'm always as good as my word."

There was the *click* of the derringer's hammer.

7

Fargo's life hung by the pressure of Barnes's trigger finger. He would have died then and there, except that Jennifer rose out of the rocking chair.

"No, you don't, girly," Barnes said, pointing the derringer at her. "None of you females are to move a muscle."

Unnoticed, Fargo slid his right hand under his pant leg and into his boot to the Arkansas toothpick nestled snug in its ankle sheath.

"If you think I won't kill a female, you're wrong," Barnes warned them. "I'm not Cord. I don't have a soft spot for petticoats."

"You're despicable, Mr. Barnes," Glenda said hotly.

"You're a fine one to talk, bitch. I know why Cord left you. You drove him to it."

"That's a bald-faced lie."

"Not hardly. He confided in me one night when he had too much to drink." Barnes was still pointing the derringer at Jennifer.

Constance hadn't moved or spoken. She seemed too scared to even blink.

"Cord Blasingame wouldn't be an outlaw if it weren't for you," Barnes said. "If you'd been a halfway good wife, he'd still be married." He paused. "When we heard you'd come here after him, some of us were all for doin' you in but he wouldn't have it."

"He has at least one redeeming quality left in him," Glenda said.

"You just don't savvy, do you? A woman can't keep a man under her heel and expect him to stay there forever. Not if he's got a lick of pride."

"What do you know, you smelly goat," Glenda said. "You'll get yours one day."

"Sooner than he thinks," Fargo said, and when Barnes glanced down, he thrust the toothpick in under his sternum, all the way to the hilt.

Billy Barnes jerked and blurted, "Hellfire!" His eyes rolled up in his head, he gave a convulsive shake, and sank into a pile.

Glenda squealed in delight.

Fargo left the blade buried. He'd stabbed men in the heart before; as soon as he pulled it out, blood would spread.

Glenda came over. "Call me a bitch, will you?" she said, and kicked the corpse in the face.

"I doubt he felt that," Fargo said.

Glenda was so mad, she kicked Barnes again. "Invade my house, will you? Call me names, will you? He got what was coming to him."

Constance finally broke her silence. "There isn't any bounty on him, is there?"

"No," Glenda said. "He's small fry."

"Stinky small fry," Jennifer said, and all three of them laughed.

Fargo was surprised at how coldhearted they were. Then again, a woman scorned could be downright mean, and by walking out on Glenda, Cord Blasingame had unleashed a she-cat. He rose and picked up his hat. "You might want to fetch some towels or rags."

"What?" Glenda said, tearing her hate-filled gaze from the body. "Oh. Yes. The blood." She gave commands to her daughters and they bustled out.

Fargo rubbed a sore spot where he'd been hit.

Placing a hand on his arm, Glenda smiled. "Thank you. He might have gotten around to hurting us, too. He never did like me. I don't think he liked women, period. Him and that Zeke."

Fargo was doing the arithmetic in his head. Blasingame plus eight men was now Blasingame plus five men. The odds were getting better. "Now you know why I wasn't in any hurry to head out."

Glenda digested that, and her eyes widened. "You figured more of them might come after you."

"Outlaws can be as loyal to each other as cowhands are loyal to a brand."

"I don't know much about cowboys," Glenda said, "except that they smell of cows."

The girls returned. Fargo offered to drag the body outside but Glenda didn't want to move it; she sent Constance to fetch the marshal.

Fargo remembered the bottle he'd put in his saddlebags and said, "I need a drink."

"You're going to the saloon at a time like this?" Glenda said in amazement.

"I have some whiskey upstairs."

"Hold on. You brought liquor into my house?"

"Do you want some?"

"I certainly do not. I don't permit it. I never allowed Cord to have any and I won't have you bringing it in, either."

"Too late." Fargo needed that drink bad. His head hurt and his ribs ached, and he could use the jolt.

"I want you to bring the bottle down and empty it."

Fargo laughed.

"I mean it."

Fargo figured he should set her straight on a few things. "You want me to track down your husband, fine. You want me to split the bounty, fine. But you don't get to boss me around. You don't tell me what to do, now or ever. And if you don't like it, send for someone else."

Glenda's face rippled with anger. "I don't deserve to be talked to like that."

"It's easy not to."

Confusion etched her face. "How do you mean?"

"Don't be a bitch."

Fargo took the stairs two at a stride. In his room he sat on the end of the bed and savored a long swallow. The burning felt good, and he smacked his lips in enjoyment. Some of the pain faded. "More medicine," he said, and chugged.

It wasn't five minutes that there came a light knock on his door. "It's me," Jennifer said.

"Come the hell in."

She had the toothpick, and held it out. "Mother said to give this to you. I wiped it clean."

"I'm obliged." Fargo hiked his pant leg and slid the knife into the sheath.

"You sure are tricky," Jennifer said.

"It keeps me breathing."

"Mother's mad at you."

"I don't give a damn." Fargo held out the bottle. "Care for a swallow?"

Jennifer stared at it longingly and licked her lips but shook her head. "She'd beat me within an inch of my life."

"Would she, now?" Fargo had come to regard Glenda Blasingame in a whole new light, and it wasn't flattering.

"Don't misunderstand," Jennifer said. "She's a good mother. She's had to work really hard to keep us fed and keep clothes on our backs."

Fargo motioned at the walls. "You have your own house."

"We rent it," Jennifer said. "We've been living off a little money she inherited when Grandma died, and it's about gone. It's why she wants the bounty money so much. If we don't get our share, I don't know what we'll do."

"But you say she beats you?"

"Now and then. Spankings, mostly, when I was little. Deep down she's a good woman trying to do the best she can."

"If you say so."

Jennifer came over and bent so her face practically touched his. "Want me to tell you a secret?"

"I'm all ears," Fargo said, although at the moment another part of him was stirring.

"Those hairs weren't hers."

"She plucked them off your goat?"

Jennifer laughed. "We don't have a goat, silly. No, they were mine." She glanced at the doorway as if to assure herself no one was there. "You see, it was my idea. We were sitting around talking about how badly we could use the bounty. Mother mentioned hearing about this famous tracker—"

"Me."

"Yes. Constance said we should send for you but Mother didn't think you'd come. She'd never heard of you tracking anyone down for money." Jennifer chuckled. "But she'd heard of your, shall we way, wanton ways? Rumor has it you're quite the ladies' man."

"I like to fuck," Fargo said.

Jennifer snorted, caught herself, and covered her mouth and nose. "I'm sorry. I think I got snot on you."

"I'll live."

"Anyway, I came up with the idea of sending you some hairs. Mother thought it was scandalous at first but Connie · and I convinced her. We figured that if you're as female hungry as they claim, you'd come running like a buck to a doe in heat."

"Hell," Fargo said.

"Mother was going to take scissors to the ends of her hair and send those but I said that you could probably tell the difference and they should be real. So I plucked my own." Jennifer laughed. "You should have seen Mother's face when we folded them up. She was red as a beet. Connie and I about laughed until we cried."

"I'd like to see the rest."

Jennifer straightened. "I can never tell when you're serious."

"I never joke about puss hairs."

"There you go again." Jennifer gave him a light smack on the arm. "And when do you think you'd like to?"

"Now is good," Fargo said, and setting down the bottle, he reached out with both hands, cupped her buttocks, and pulled her to him. He pressed his face to her nether mount and nuzzled her through her dress.

Jennifer gasped and arched her back. "Oh God!" she gasped, and made as if to push him away. Instead, she suddenly grabbed his head and pushed his face harder into her.

Fargo could feel the slope of her mount and the warmth of her thighs. He kneaded her bottom with one hand while raising the other to a breast and cupping it.

"Ohhhhhh," Jennifer husked.

Fargo's member was swelling into a redwood. He stood and kissed her and she hungrily tried to suck his tongue down her throat.

Mewing like a kitten, Jennifer placed her hand on his pole. She pulled back, looked down, and her mouth formed an O. "I had no idea."

"Want to see it?" Fargo said, and was about to undo his buckle when steps sounded on the stairs and someone came hurrying down the hall.

Quickly stepping back, Jennifer smoothed her dress and fluffed at her hair.

Fargo picked up the whiskey bottle and held it in front of him to hide his bulge.

Constance bustled in. "Sorry to bother you," she said, "but the marshal is here and he wants to see Mr. Fargo."

"Wonderful," Fargo said.

8

The lawman was crouched by the body, probing at the wound with his fingertips. "I see you stabbed him," he said as Fargo entered the parlor.

"Nothing gets past you, does it?" Fargo said.

He sat in the rocking chair and tilted the bottle to his lips.

Glenda frowned in disapproval. "I wish you wouldn't do that in front of my girls."

"Do what?" Marshal Cripdin asked, and glanced at Fargo. "Oh. Well, there's no law against that. There is against killing, though, and Billy Barnes is definitely dead."

"You are a wonderment," Fargo said.

Cripdin stood. "Mrs. Hemmings tells me you killed him in self-defense. That he barged in here determined to kill you for shooting Zeke Bell."

"It's been one of those days."

"I'll say it has," Cripdin declared. "In less than twelve hours you've killed three of the worst outlaws in the territory."

"Lucky me."

"You won't think that when Cord Blasingame comes after you. Be smart and light a shuck before there's more killing."

"Can't," Fargo said.

"Why in Hades not? What's keeping you here?"

Fargo avoided looking at Glenda. "I have something to do."

"What?" the lawman demanded, and when Fargo didn't answer, he snapped, "I asked you a question, damn you."

Fargo set the bottle of Monongahela on the floor and slowly stood. He towered a good half foot over Cripdin, who gave a noticeable start. "Talk to me like that again."

"Now see here," Cripdin said.

"Marshal," Glenda broke in, "I'd be ever so pleased if you would remove the body. You can't expect to leave it here all night."

"What? Oh." Cripdin appeared grateful for the excuse to get out of there. "You're right. It wouldn't be fitting. I'll go fetch some men to help and we'll have it removed inside the hour." Smiling, he touched his hat brim and hurried off.

"Why, he was scared silly," Jennifer said.

"Hush. He might hear you," Glenda cautioned. She waited for the sound of the front door closing to say, "But you're right. He was." Kneeling, she did something Fargo realized he should have done; she went through Barnes's pockets. He had a poke with forty-two dollars, some lucifers, a few spare cartridges for his Sharps, and a scrap of paper. She was about to drop the paper on the pile when she set it on the floor and smoothed it out. "What's this?"

Fargo picked up the Monongahela and went over.

The paper had been torn from a tablet, and on it someone had drawn a crude likeness of a bird's head.

"What do you make of it?"

Fargo swallowed whiskey, and shrugged.

"You don't seem interested. It could be important."

"I'm tired," Fargo said, and he was. Rising, he took the paper and stuffed it into a pocket. "I'm going to bed. If the marshal needs to talk to me, tell him it'll have to wait until morning." He nodded at each of the girls and bent his steps up the stairs.

Fargo didn't bother undressing. He tossed his hat on the

chest of drawers, removed his spurs, took off his gun belt and placed it beside his pillow, blew out the lamp, and sprawled onto the bed. It was so soft, the room so warm and cozy, that in no time he drifted off. His sleep was undisturbed—until suddenly he was awake with no idea why.

Fargo lay still, listening. The house was quiet. He opened his eyes. The bedroom was dark save for faint starlight around the edges of the curtains. Without moving his head he glanced at the door; he couldn't be sure, but he thought it was open.

It had been closed when he turned in.

Easing his hand to his holster, Fargo slid the Colt out. He didn't cock it. If someone was there, they'd hear.

Something rustled, and a silhouette appeared at the foot of the bed.

For all Fargo knew, it was another outlaw out for revenge. He coiled to spring, and caught a whiff of perfume. "Who's there?" he growled.

The figure came around the bed, and bent. A finger was pressed to his lips. "Shhhh. It's me. We don't want Mother to hear." Jennifer whispered. She removed her finger.

"What do you want?" Fargo asked, although he had a good idea.

"It's past two," Jennifer whispered. "Mother and Connie are asleep."

Fargo's eyes were adjusting. He could make out the cotton robe she wore. "That doesn't answer my question."

"I want more," Jennifer whispered.

"Of what?"

"What do you think?"

"And you left the door open so anyone can walk in on us?"

"Oh Lordy." Jennifer scooted over to it.

Fargo sat up and leaned back against the headboard. He pushed his gun belt under a pillow and stretched out his legs.

"I'm back," Jennifer whispered.

Fargo patted the bed. "Climb on."

"First you have to promise me something."

"I won't bite your nipples off."

"What? No. Not that. I want your word that you won't tell my mother."

"Damn. I was going to wake her up and boast about it as soon as we're done."

"Be serious." Jennifer slid onto the bed but stayed half a foot away and didn't touch him.

She stared for so long that Fargo said, "Are you waiting for Christmas?"

"I don't have a lot of experience," Jennifer said in a small voice. "Isn't it the man who should start things?"

"Where are my manners?" Fargo said. Smiling, he pulled her close so they were chest to breast. "I'll take it easy on you." Which, now that he thought about it, was a good idea; too much noise and they'd wake Glenda and there'd be hell to pay.

He kissed her and she nibbled at his lips as if they were cake. He covered a firm breast and she cooed and her nipple became a tack. Parting the robe with his other hand, he ran it over her belly.

Jennifer's hands swooped to his pants. She unfastened the buckle and with almost frantic urgency, pushed and pried his pants down to get at him. He shifted and suddenly her fingers were on his member, stroking him. A lump formed in his throat, and it was all he could do to breathe. She fondled and cupped him, low down. For someone so green, she knew just what to do. He had to will himself not to explode.

Together, they stretched out. He peeled her robe off and she tugged his buckskin shirt over his head.

Jennifer kissed his ears, his neck. She licked his throat. She rained small kisses on his shoulders and his ribs.

Fargo grew hot all over. He craved her as he earlier had

craved a drink. Kneading first one melon and then the other, he pinched and pulled on her nipples, causing her to squirm and moan. He ran his fingernails down her back and she shivered. When he caressed her thighs, her legs parted of their own accord.

Fargo was about to slide between them when he heard a sound out in the hall. He froze, his hand poised to delve to her nether mount.

"What?" Jennifer whispered. "Why did you stop?"

"Something," Fargo answered. He cocked his head, listening. He wasn't sure what the sound had been. A scratching sound, he thought. "Do you have a cat?"

"No. My mother hates them."

"A dog?"

"Did you see one?"

"Maybe someone else is up," Fargo whispered. He could just see Glenda barging in and tearing into him for having his way with her daughter.

"They were sleeping like logs, I tell you." Jennifer raised her own head and after half a minute said, "You're imagining things."

Fargo reckoned that maybe he'd been mistaken. It didn't occur to him until he resumed kissing and caressing her that another outlaw might be out to get him. Three had tried already. Who was to say a fourth wouldn't?

The notion bothered him so much, he couldn't bring himself to relax and enjoy their lovemaking. A part of him was alert for more sounds or anything else out of the ordinary.

He massaged one leg and then the other. But he didn't touch her where it would excite her the most until she was panting with need and husked into his ear, "Please. Oh, please."

Fargo placed his hand on her slit. She was hot and wet. He ran a finger along it and she arched into him and sank her teeth into his shoulder.

Fargo cut the foreplay short. He couldn't shake the feeling that someone was out there. Whoever it was must be listening. Jennifer and he were being quiet but it was still obvious what they were doing.

"Why did you stop?"

Fargo hadn't realized he had.

"Did you hear something again?"

"No."

"Am I boring you then?"

"You talk too much." Rising onto his knees, Fargo aligned his member, inserted the tip, and slid inch by gradual inch up into her.

Gasping, Jennifer dug her fingernails into both of his arms.

Fargo only had to stroke a few times and he had a wildcat under him.

"Oh! Oh!"

Jennifer exploded with a ferocity that caught him off guard. The bed shook and the headboard thumped the wall and he inwardly cursed the noise they were making.

Then it was his turn, and he didn't much care. He rammed up into her fit to tear her apart. His explosion rivaled hers.

Afterward, they lay spent and slick with sweat.

Fargo rolled off to spare her his weight and she bundled the robe about her and sat up.

"Thank you," she whispered. "I'd better get back to my room."

"Any time," Fargo drowsily responded.

"And see?" Jennifer teased. "Nothing happened. No one was out there."

That was when the Ovaro whinnied.

9

Fargo heard it even with the window closed. He knew the stallion as well as he knew himself, knew the sounds it made, and the whinny told him something was amiss.

He was off the bed before the whinny died. Pulling his pants up, he slid his hand under the pillow and grabbed his gun belt.

"What is it?" Jennifer asked in alarm.

"Get to your room." Fargo didn't bother with his shirt or his hat. Racing out the door and along the hall, he bounded down the stairs.

The house was dark and quiet. He reached the kitchen, threw the bolt on the back door and gripped the latch, and caught himself. It could be another outlaw. To go rushing out was the worst mistake he could make.

Cautious now, he moved to a window. He could see the Ovaro over by the fence. It was staring into the night, its ears pricked.

Quickly, Fargo opened the door wide enough to slip out. The air was cool on his skin. Crouching, he ran to the stallion and stared in the same direction.

An empty lot bordered the property on that side. It was choked with grass and weeds that waved gently in the wind.

Fargo waited. If someone was out there, eventually they'd give themselves away. He heard voices in the house, and light flared in an upstairs window. Intent on the lot, he didn't think more of it until more light spilled from the back doorway.

"Fargo?"

Wearing a bulky woolen robe tied at the waist, Glenda was holding a small lamp. "What are you doing? What was all the ruckus?"

Fargo was caught in the lamp's glow, an easy target. But no shots boomed. Retreating to the house, he ushered her inside and closed the door behind them.

"What is it?"

Jennifer and Constance were over by the hall, Constance nervously gnawing her lip.

"Something was out there," Fargo said. Something, or some*one*. "It spooked my horse."

"Is it gone?"

"I think so."

Glenda set the lamp on the kitchen table. "It could have been a coyote. They come into town from time to time."

"Once a bear did," Jennifer said.

"And there are skunks," Constance threw in.

Fargo hadn't caught the scent of a polecat and he doubted it was a bear or any other animal. He had a sense that it was a man, although why he was so sure, he couldn't say. "Sorry I woke you."

"It's perfectly all right," Glenda said. "After what happened with Barnes, we can't be too careful."

It occurred to Fargo that, "Your husband must know I'm staying here."

"My former husband," Glenda stressed. "He's nothing to me now. He lost all claim to my affections when he ran out on us."

Jennifer came over, her arms folded around her breasts. "What if he came back and begged your forgiveness?"

"You've asked that before," Glenda said, "and my answer is still the same. I want nothing more to do with him, ever."

Constance said, "I wish things could be like they were before he left. I miss him."

"I'd rather we talked about something else," Glenda told them.

"You're just mad because he walked out," Jennifer said.

"Of course I'm mad. Any grown woman would be."

"If you took him back," Constance said, "we could be a family again."

"Will the two of you stop it?" Glenda said. "Wishful thinking never does anyone any good. My marriage ended the day he abandoned us."

Fargo wasn't about to stand there and listen to them bicker. "Ladies," he said, moving past the table. "I need more sleep. I'll be leaving right after breakfast."

"To where?" Glenda asked. "You have no idea where Cord is."

True, but Fargo had an idea how he might find out. After the bushwhacking at the pass, he wasn't entirely sure he could trust the three of them. Which reminded him. He stopped and looked back. "Who did you three tell?"

"I beg your pardon?" Glenda said.

"Who knew you sent for me?"

"No one. We've kept it a secret. Just as no one knows I'm Cord's wife."

"Not even the marshal?"

"Cripdin?" Glenda said, and laughed. "That oaf. He couldn't keep a secret if his life depended on it. He's the last person I'd tell." She paused. "Why do you ask?"

Fargo shrugged. It was better they not know he suspected one of them. With a bob of his head to Jennifer and Constance, he returned to his room. He closed the door, plopped onto the bed, and pondered until he drifted into a fitful sleep.

As was his habit, he was up before sunrise. He washed in the basin, dressed, and went out to saddle the Ovaro.

A pink blush heralded the new day. Already the birds were in song, and somewhere a cat mewed.

Clatter in the kitchen greeted him. Glenda was getting out pots and pans. "Morning," she said. "I figured you'd want to leave early. I've already kindled the stove and put coffee on." She opened a cupboard. "How many eggs would you like? And how do you like them?"

When on the trail Fargo seldom ate breakfast; he treated himself. "Six should do me. Scrambled."

Glenda laid out slices of bacon in a frying pan, then broke eggs into another. She made toast, too, and set out jam.

Jennifer joined them as her mother was setting out plates. She wore a bright blue dress and had tied her hair back with a matching ribbon and looked fresh-scrubbed and happy. "Morning, everyone."

"My, aren't you in a good mood," Glenda said. "Normally you're a grump this early in the day. I take it you slept well after our little disturbance?"

"Nothing little about it," Jennifer said with a secret wink at Fargo. "But yes, I slept better than I have in ages."

Constance shuffled in, still in a robe. "The smells woke me up," she said, stifling a yawn.

"Go back upstairs and get dressed," Glenda said. "We have company."

"It's only him," Constance said, with a nod at Fargo. "He saw me like this last night."

"That's not the point."

"If you insist," Constance grumbled, making it sound as if it were the greatest inconvenience ever inflicted on a human being.

Fargo took his time eating. He'd be in the saddle most of the day, and who knew how many days after. Little was said. Constance was sullen. Glenda seemed to be thinking hard about something. As for Jennifer, she'd give him sly smiles when she thought her mother and sister weren't looking.

By eight Fargo was in the saddle.

"I still don't see what you hope to accomplish," Glenda remarked. "Not when you don't have a clue where he is."

"He knows where I am," Fargo said.

"Don't let anything happen to you if you can help it. I'm counting on you for my half of the bounty."

"Nice to know you care," Fargo said.

A jab of his spurs, and he rode down the main street to the north end of Meridian. Beyond, he passed isolated cabins. At one a dog barked. At another children waved.

He never once looked back. If he was right, it wouldn't do to let on that he suspected.

The road ended at the edge of forest that stretched on forever. He went a dozen yards in and drew rein. It wasn't long before a rider appeared. To say he was surprised was putting it mildly. It wasn't an outlaw.

Dismounting, he walked the Ovaro behind a blue spruce, shucked the Henry from the saddle scabbard, and waited to show himself until hooves clomped on the carpet of pine needles.

Leveling the Henry as he stepped into the open, Fargo said, "Well, look who it is."

Marshal Theodore Cripdin jerked on his reins. "You!" he blurted. He blinked, then asked, "What are you doing here?"

"Waiting for you."

Cripdin switched his reins from one hand to the other. "How can that be? I decided to go for a ride on the spur of the moment."

"Bullshit," Fargo said. "You're following me."

"Why would I do that?"

"For Blasingame."

"You're loco." Cripdin tapped his badge. "I'm not part of his gang."

"You were watching Glenda's house last night."

"I did no such thing," Cripdin said. "I was home in bed."

"Why don't I believe you?" Fargo asked. "You wouldn't

be the first tin star I've come across who isn't worthy to wear a badge."

"Now see here," Cripdin blustered. "You might not think much of me but I'm honest."

"Yet here you are."

"I'm out for a ride, I tell you."

Fargo raised the Henry to his shoulder. "Here's how it will be. You'll turn around and go back to town. If Blasingame asks, tell him I was on to you and didn't leave you any choice."

"You think you know everything but you don't."

"If I catch you following me again," Fargo warned, "I won't be this nice."

"I'm the one friend you have, mister."

"In that case," Fargo said, "I don't want any. Light a shuck unless you want to be shot."

"You wouldn't kill a law officer," Cripdin said. "I have half a mind to call your bluff."

"Who's bluffing?" Fargo said, and thumbed back the hammer.

Cripdin puffed out his cheeks and glowered. "I resent this. Here I thought I was doing you a favor and you pull this stunt."

"Favor?" Fargo scoffed.

"Keeping an eye on you in case Blasingame's gang tried to bury you."

"You expect me to believe that?"

"I don't care what you believe," Cripdin said. "I'm washing my hands of you. I've tried to help and you won't let me." He started to rein around to ride off, or pretended to—his other hand dropped to his six-shooter.

10

Fargo trained the Henry on him and said, "How stupid are you?"

Cripdin froze. "I should put you behind bars is what I should do."

"Take your goddamn hand off that smoke wagon," Fargo said.

The lawman jerked it off and splayed his fingers. "There. Happy?"

"You're the dumbest son of a bitch I've met in a coon's age."

"I'm the *law*. And I'm tired of you treating me with disrespect."

"Go back to town. You get this one warning and this one warning only. The next time you try to pull one on me, it will end different."

"You have no respect for the law."

"No," Fargo said. "I have no respect for you."

Cripdin's face twitched, and for a few moments Fargo thought he would go for his six-gun. But Cripdin only growled, "From here on out you're on your own."

"I always was."

Reining around, Cripdin took out his anger on his horse by jabbing his spurs. The animal broke into a gallop and soon all that was left of them was the dust the horse had raised.

Fargo moved to a pine and sat with his back to the trunk. Crossing his legs, he placed the Henry across them, and waited.

Apparently he'd been mistaken. He'd thought for sure that another outlaw was watching and waiting a turn to try to kill him. But maybe, just maybe, the lawman was telling the truth. It could have been Cripdin last night who made the Ovaro whinny, and now had followed him to make sure he wasn't bushwhacked.

The more he thought about it, though, the more convinced he was that his initial hunch was right. Someone else was out there, stalking him. He'd learned a long time ago to trust his instincts; they'd saved his hide more than once.

He let about half an hour go by. Just when he was convinced he had been wrong and no one was coming, a horse and rider appeared in the distance. One second they weren't there; the next they were. The instant he set eyes on them, the rider drew rein.

Fargo didn't move, didn't so much as twitch. Whoever it was, the rider sat dappled in shadow, studying the woods.

The minutes crawled, and still the rider didn't move. Finally he came on at a slow walk and crossed a patch of sunlight.

It was a half-breed, as folks would say, a mix of white and Indian. In his case his features showed more of the latter than the former.

Fargo couldn't tell exactly which tribe. He remembered Tassy at the saloon saying that one of the outlaws who rode with Blasingame was a breed.

Stockily built, the man wore a bandanna tied round his long black hair, a brown shirt and pants. A bandoleer was slanted across his chest, half filled with cartridges for the Spencer he held. He favored Apache-style knee-high moccasins. Several times he bent down, apparently reading the sign.

Fargo continued to stay perfectly still. The breed wouldn't be like most men; any movement, he'd spot it right away.

The breed stopped again and intently scanned the trees. It was obvious he suspected something wasn't right.

Fargo admired the man's instincts. They were a lot like his own.

The breed's dark eyes roved every which way. Suddenly he stiffened. He wasn't looking at Fargo. He was staring at the tree Fargo had hidden the Ovaro behind.

Fargo brought the Henry up but already the breed was hauling on his reins. He fixed a quick bead and fired and knew he'd missed.

The breed's bay was quick. In moments they were out of sight.

Leaping erect, Fargo ran to the Ovaro. He vaulted into the saddle and gave chase. He came to the road and spied tendrils of dust and raced to the first bend and around.

The breed wasn't in sight. Nor was there any dust.

Fargo brought the stallion to a stop and rose in the stirrups. He listened but heard nothing so he bent to read the tracks.

In the forest on the right side of the road a rifle spanged and lead sizzled a whisker's-width above Fargo's hat.

Fargo charged into the undergrowth. He went a short way and stopped. He listened but heard only the breeze.

Sooner or later the man would move and Fargo would pinpoint his position. He stayed still five, ten, fifteen minutes. No sounds broke the stillness. He figured the breed must be doing the same thing. Then he happened to lift his gaze to the slopes above, and there, in a clearing out of rifle range, stood the bay.

The breed raised a hand as if in salute, reined around, and rode off up the mountain.

"I'll be damned," Fargo said. It was rare for anyone to get the better of him. The breed was slick, an equal if not a better.

He went after him. He climbed to the clearing and found the bay's tracks and followed them to the crest of the mountain, where they vanished.

Fargo searched in ever widening circles and couldn't find so much as a partial hoofprint. It was as if the breed and the bay had melted into thin air. "I'll be damned," he said, and smiled.

With one eye always on his back trail, Fargo descended the mountain and made for Meridian. The breed didn't reappear.

It was the middle of the afternoon when he reached town. He didn't go to Glenda's; he tied the Ovaro off at the hitch rail in front of the Ace's High.

A couple of townsmen were playing poker and an old man was at the end of the bar deep in his cups.

Fargo paid for a bottle and claimed the same corner table as before. He'd barely filled his glass when who should come sashaying out of a hall at the back but Tassy. Today she had on a red dress that had to be two sizes too small. She came to his table and without being asked pulled out a chair.

"Mind some company?"

"Thought you were mad at me."

"For a little bit I was. But you're too handsome to stay mad at for long."

"Me and all the other handsome fellas."

"Don't start." Tassy nodded at the bottle. "How about buying a girl breakfast?"

Fargo pushed the glass across and was considerably impressed when she chugged it in a single gulp. "Damn, woman."

"I bet you could do the same." Tassy pushed the glass back. "A refill, if you please."

Fargo obliged her. This time she sipped it and studied him. "Something on your mind?" he asked.

"No," Tassy said, and uttered a light laugh. "Just admiring your good looks."

Fargo swirled the liquor in the bottle and took a long drink. "You're right," he said. "Nothing like whiskey to perk a body up."

Tassy winked. "You don't look like you need too much perking."

"I ran into a friend of yours earlier," Fargo remarked, setting the bottle down.

"Oh?"

"That breed you were telling me about."

"You met Niyan?"

"Is that his name?"

"Part of it," Tassy said. "The part whites can pronounce." She rimmed the top of her glass with a fingertip. "You must be good, mister, if you ran into him and you're still breathing."

"We played hide and seek. He won."

"Listen, handsome," Tassy said, "if he's out to get you, sooner or later he will. You want my advice? You'll make yourself scarce while you can."

"Tuck tail and run?" Fargo grinned. "What do you take me for?"

"Smart," Tassy said. "Tangling with Niyan is dumb. He's killed more men than you have fingers and toes."

"How would you know that?"

"Ask around. Everyone says he has."

"Ah, well, if everyone says it, it must be true."

Tassy shook her head. "God Almighty, you're—what's the word? Cynical. That's the one. You're cynical as hell."

"I have my cynical moments," Fargo agreed. He took another swig. "I have my randy moments, too."

"Do you, now?" Tassy replied with a smirk.

"I'm having one at the moment," Fargo said. He didn't tell her he wanted to question her about Cord Blasingame and his gang, and he figured she'd be more open about it after she'd gushed a few times.

"This early?" Tassy said.

"When a man has to fuck," Fargo said, "a man has to fuck."

Tassy laughed and sipped and coughed. "I know I said I'd never let you poke me but I was angry at the time. I felt as if you were picking on me. Truth is, I wouldn't fight you off."

"I wouldn't fight you off, either."

Tassy laughed.

"My place or yours?" Fargo said, and snapped his fingers. "Wait. I don't have a place."

"Mine it is. Although I hear you've taken a room with the Hemmingses."

"I have," Fargo admitted since it would be pointless to lie. "And one of her rules is no getting sweat on her sheets."

"That sounds like her. But you can get all the sweat you want on my sheets."

"Lead on, madam."

"You sure are playful. I hope you're the same once our clothes are off."

"There's one way to find out."

Her boardinghouse was a block from the saloon. A sign said that all the rooms were taken.

"Mine's on the top floor," Tassy informed him. "And hide that bottle. If the landlady sees it, she'll have a fit."

Fargo held it against his side until they'd climbed to her room and she'd opened her door and motioned for him to go in. "Care for some?"

"No, thanks." Tassy closed the door and stood with her back to him, her head bowed.

"Something the matter?"

"Yes." Tassy turned.

In her right hand was a knife.

11

"What the hell?"

Fargo barely got the words out of his mouth when Tassy hissed like a kicked rattler and came at him swinging. Her first swing struck the whiskey bottle and sent it flying; the bottle struck a wall and shattered.

Her second swing nearly took his fingers off.

Retreating, Fargo sidestepped a stab at his ribs. He took another step back and collided with a small table. The next he knew, he was flat on his back.

"I won't let you!" Tassy shrieked, and threw herself on top of him.

Fargo grabbed her wrist as the knife sheared at his neck. Cursing, she clawed at his face with her other hand, trying to rake his eyes. She missed and ripped open his cheek instead.

Her attack had caught him flat-footed but now Fargo was mad. He flung her off and she came down on her knees. As she whipped her arm overhead to stab him in the chest, he kicked her in the gut. She cried out and doubled over, giving him time to scramble to his feet.

"I won't let you!" she wailed again, and swung at his legs.

Fargo dodged.

Tassy's fury was a sight to behold. She was beside herself, her eyes flames of hate, her teeth bared like a rabid animal's.

Fargo was lucky in one respect. She had no skill at knife-fighting. Where a seasoned fighter would have gone for his vitals with quick stabs that would be hard to block or evade, she came at him like a windmill gone berserk. She slashed high, she slashed low. She tried to kick him in the knee to slow him.

Fargo felt his back hit a wall. He twisted aside as the blade swept at his throat and heard it thunk into the wood. Diving, he grabbed hold of the small table by two of its legs. He turned as she did, and when she lunged, he whipped the table up and around.

The crash was loud in the small room. It struck her on the head and the left shoulder.

Tassy cried out and sprawled flat.

Fargo sucked in deep breaths. He was breathing as if he had run a mile. Hunkering, he felt for a pulse. It was strong; she'd live but she had a nasty gash on her forehead, and she was bleeding.

She still clenched the knife.

Wresting it from her grasp, Fargo cuts strips from the bottom of her dress and bound her wrists and her ankles. He wedged the knife under his belt, moved to a pitcher on a counter, and filled a glass with water. He took a few swallows, then stood over Tassy and upended it onto her face.

Sputtering and coughing, she opened her eyes. She tried to sit up, realized she was bound, and cursed him anew.

Moving to a settee, Fargo sat and touched the scratch marks on his cheeks. They weren't deep but they stung like hell.

"Serves you right," Tassy growled. "Wish I'd blinded you."

"Was that your idea of lovemaking?"

"You bastard," Tassy spat. "Did you think I'd let you get away with it?"

"With screwing you?"

"With killing Cord Blasingame!" Tassy wriggled toward him. "I'll bite your neck open if I can reach you. So help me."

"Damn, woman," Fargo said. She snapped at his leg and he kicked her in the side. "You mind explaining what this is all about?"

"Isn't it plain?" Tassy spat. "I won't have you hurt Cord. It's bad enough you've killed Clemens, Zeke and Barnes. They were good men."

"They were outlaws."

"They were good outlaws."

"Are you drunk?" Fargo asked, only half in jest, and had to jerk his legs to one side when she rammed her feet at him. "Do that once more and I'll hit you with the table and not hold back."

"You would, wouldn't you? You're the meanest son of a bitch I've ever met."

"Says the bitch who tried to cut me."

"How many times do I have to say it? You had it coming. Riding into town like you're God Almighty and killing my friends."

"Ah," Fargo said.

"Don't 'ah' me," Tassy said. "You have no right. Especially Cord. He's the nicest fella I know. And yes, I'm sweet on him."

"I never would have guessed," Fargo said.

"I hate you."

Fargo sat back. "So Cord Blasingame is the nicest man you know?"

"My exact words," Tassy said with a nod, "and I stand by them."

"Is this the same Cord Blasingame who has a bounty on his head for killing and robbing?"

"It is."

"Sure sounds like a nice gent to me."

"You son of a bitch. What do you know?" Tassy closed her eyes and groaned. "Damn. You have me all worked up. And my head is pounding like hell."

"Where's a towel?" Fargo asked. "I'll clean off the blood."

"Don't do me no favors."

"I've already done you one," Fargo said. "I let you live."

A scarlet drop trickled down Tassy's nose to the very tip. "I can't wait for one of the others to kill you. They'll protect him with their lives if need be, just like me."

Fargo absorbed that and said, "You're saying that the outlaws I've tangled with weren't out to kill me because I'm after the bounty? They want me dead so I can't hurt Cord?"

"You finally caught on, you dumb bastard."

"Lady, one of us is loco and it's not me."

Tassy was livid. She was so mad, she shook as if having a fit, then snarled, "Mark my words. All of us would die rather than let you harm him. Why do you think they follow him so devotedly? Cord Blasingame is a special human being."

"I'll be sure to mention that when I catch up to him," Fargo said.

To his amazement she broke into tears and cried in great racking sobs, her brow pressed to the floor.

Fargo waited for it to end. She had him puzzled and he'd like a few answers. The portrait she painted of Blasingame didn't fit what Glenda had told him.

Tassy wept until she was spent. She lay curled on her side and sniffled and wouldn't look at him.

"Can we talk?" Fargo asked.

"Go to hell."

"I'm trying to savvy all this."

"Don't strain that pea you use for a brain."

"Cord Blasingame has robbed the Meridian bank. Yes or no?"

"His gang did, yes," Tassy said, and sniffled some more.

"He's robbed stages?"

"His gang has, yes."

"Why do you keeping saying his gang and not him? He's their leader."

"It's not so much he leads as they follow."

"That makes no kind of sense," Fargo said. He was growing irritated.

"It would if you knew Cord like I know him."

"How is that, exactly?"

"He came into the saloon one night a few years ago and we hit it off. He wasn't like most men. He was kind and considerate and treated me like a lady." Tassy raised her head to glare. Her eyes were wet and puffy and snot was running from her nose. "He wasn't at all like some men I could mention."

"You're still not making sense," Fargo said. "How can he do all that robbing and lead a pack of killers and be the nicest gent alive?"

"I've said all I'm going to." She clamped her mouth shut and averted her face.

"Fine," Fargo said. He knew a lost cause when he saw one. Rising, he stepped to the door.

"Hold on, damn you," Tassy said. "You're not fixing to leave me trussed like this?"

"I cut you free, you'll grab another knife and come at me."

"I give you my word I won't. I've learned my lesson. Believe me."

"I wouldn't trust you if my life depended on it," Fargo said, "and it does." Taking her knife from under his belt, he set it on the floor by the door. "After I'm gone, crawl over here and cut yourself loose. It shouldn't take more than half an hour or so."

"Bastard."

"There you go again, heaping on the sweet talk." Fargo opened the door. "Remember. You come at me again, I won't be as nice as your wonderful Cord."

"If the roof were to fall on you, I'd whoop for joy."

Fargo got out of there. He stood out in the street, contemplating, and finally bent his boots to the marshal's office.

Theodore Cripdin was behind his desk, writing. He

looked up as the door opened and snapped, "What the hell do you want?"

"I sure am popular," Fargo said.

"Not with me you're not. Not after how you treated me. Get out of my office before I throw you out."

Fargo sat on the edge of the lawman's desk. "Tell me about Cord Blasingame."

"Didn't you hear me?"

"How nice is he?"

Cripdin blinked and set down his pencil. "Who have you been talking to? He doesn't like that to get around."

"Has he or has he not killed people?"

"He hasn't."

Fargo was good at reading people. He had to be, as much poker as he played. And his instincts told him the marshal was telling the truth. "Has he or has he not robbed people?"

"Sort of," Cripdin said.

"How the hell do you 'sort of' rob somebody?"

"His men did the robbing. He just rode along with them."

"But they're *his* men?"

"Sort of. They follow him."

"Is everyone in this damn town short of common sense?" Fargo stood and leaned on the desk. "I want the truth about why you were following me this morning. Were you really out to keep his men from hurting me?"

Cripdin folded his hands and shook his head. "I reckon I might as well own up to it. No, I wasn't out to keep them from hurting you." He paused. "I was out to keep you from hurting him."

12

The marshal refused to say any more so Fargo left. He needed a drink. He went to the Ace's High and bought another bottle. As the bartender placed it in front of him he said, "I'd like to ask you a question."

The barkeep was rake thin and mostly bald and liked to chew on toothpicks. "So long as it's not personal, go ahead."

"Cord Blasingame."

"I hear tell you're huntin' him."

"Have you met him?"

"I've served him drinks right where you're standin'."

"What kind of man is he?"

The barman scrunched up his face in thought and answered, "The salt of the earth."

"He's an *outlaw*."

"So? That doesn't mean he's bad or mean or anything. Truth is, if he wasn't an outlaw, he'd make a damn fine parson, he's so nice."

"There's that word again," Fargo said in disgust.

"I don't know why you're mad at me," the bartender said. "You asked."

Fargo paid and gripped the bottle by the neck and started to turn.

"I will tell you this, mister," the man said. "You harm a hair on his head and some folks in these parts will want to take you out and string you up."

Fargo wasn't in the best of moods as he climbed on the Ovaro and rode up the street to the Hemmingses'. He noticed people staring and their looks weren't friendly.

He rode around to the back of the house and looped the reins in the fence. Striding to the back door, he entered without knocking.

Glenda was at the stove, stirring a large pot. "You're back!" she exclaimed. "How did it go today? Did you find any sign of Cord?"

Fargo pulled out a chair and sat at the table. He opened the bottle, swallowed, and coughed. "You were his wife?"

Glenda stopped stirring. "I've already told you that. So?"

"For how long?"

"Let's see. He left me about five years ago so I guess we were married pretty near sixteen. Why?"

"You must know him really well," Fargo said.

"Better than anyone, I'd imagine," Glenda boasted. "Again, why do you ask?"

"What kind of man is he?"

"He's the meanest bastard who ever drew breath," Glenda declared. "He has a heart of ice and the temperament of a wolf."

Fargo stared.

"What?" Glenda asked. "If you don't mind my saying, you're acting strangely."

"Care for a drink?" Fargo said, and wagged the bottle.

Glenda hesitated, but only for a few moments. Stepping to a cupboard, she took down a glass and came over. She poured, filling the glass about a third fill. "I don't usually drink this time of the day." Her sip barely wet her lips.

"Where are your girls?"

"We needed a few groceries so I sent them shopping." Glenda indicated the pot. "We're having stew for supper, if that's all right."

"Food is food," Fargo said. When he'd lived with the

Sioux and stayed with other tribes, he'd eaten things that most whites would turn up their noses at.

"I've baked a pie for dessert."

Fargo thought he'd smelled baked apples. "I'll be leaving again tomorrow," he announced. "To go up into the mountains. I might be gone for several days."

"You'll take us with you so we can be the bait?"

"No."

"How will you find him? It'll be like looking for a needle in a haystack. Why not wait until Cord robs somebody and pick up his trail then?"

"I want to look around," Fargo said. "Get the lay of the land." He'd never been to the Shadow Mountains before, whereas Blasingame must know them like the back of his hand.

"That makes sense, I suppose," Glenda said. "But you be careful. Anything happens to you, I lose my half of the bounty money."

"It's nice to know you care," Fargo said dryly.

"I like you. I truly do. But make no mistake. This is a business arrangement. We're in this together for the money."

"I'd almost forgotten," Fargo said.

"How can you forget five thousand dollars? For me it will be a dream come true. No more scraping by for me and my girls."

"Did Cord treat you decent?" Fargo bluntly asked.

Glenda pursed her lips. "That's a peculiar thing to want to know. But yes, I'd say the early years of our marriage, he did. We got along really well until right before the end. Which is why I was so shocked when he walked out."

"But you just said he's the meanest bastard alive."

"For walking out on me, he is. For deserting his own children." Glenda swirled the whiskey in her glass. "Only a man with a heart of ice could do that."

Fargo grunted. Something wasn't adding up.

"I wish you'd reconsider about taking us along. It will draw him in as surely as anything."

"It could get you and your girls killed."

"Cord would never harm a hair on our heads. I'd feel perfectly safe."

"Even though he's the meanest bastard who ever drew breath?"

"Why are you harping on that? He's not like most people. He's . . . complicated."

"He's something," Fargo said.

Voices and laughter peeled at the front of the house, and down the hall came Jennifer and Constance. Glenda rose to greet them and relieve them of the groceries.

Jennifer came over and with her back to her mother and sister, puckered her lips as if kissing him. "How has your day been, Mr. Fargo?"

"Complicated," Fargo said.

"Would you care to see the town with me? I'd like to go for a stroll."

"Don't bother him, dear," Glenda said. "He's been off most of the day and must be tired."

"Are you too tired to . . . stroll?" Jennifer asked, and only Fargo saw her glance at his crotch and the carnal gleam that came into her pretty eyes.

"I'm never too tired for that. If your mother doesn't mind."

Glenda was opening a container of salt. "No, I guess not. There's not much left to fix for supper. Be back here in half an hour, you hear?"

"I'd like to go," Constance said.

"And leave your poor mother to finish getting the meal ready on her own?" Glenda said. "But very well. It isn't fair that Jennifer gets to and you don't."

Jennifer frowned. "Sure, sis. Come along."

The street was quiet at that time of the day. Most women

were home doing what Glenda was doing. Most men were getting ready to close their businesses as soon as the sun went down.

Several of the people who were out and about gave Fargo the look he'd been getting all day. He didn't care. He ambled along with the girls on either side of him.

Jennifer noticed the stares and along about the third time she remarked, "You don't seem to be very popular."

"Your father is," Fargo said.

Constance brightened. "People always take to him. He has a way about him."

"When he's not robbing banks and stages."

"Even then. He's always been very well liked. He once told me that he had so many friends, he couldn't count them all."

"The hell you say," Fargo said.

"What's wrong?" Constance asked.

"How do you two feel about me going after him?"

The sisters glanced at one another and Jennifer answered, "We argued with Mother about it."

"We never wanted to come here in the first place," Constance said. "She should leave him be."

"She wants the money," Jennifer said.

"And you two don't?"

Constance fiddled with her sleeve. "It would be nice to have some for a change. I won't deny that. But not if it means Father ends up behind bars for the rest of his days."

"We want to talk to you about that," Jennifer said. "The bounty is for dead or alive. We'd like that you not kill him."

Constance nodded. "Please, Mr. Fargo. Bring him back alive, for our sakes."

"It would crush us having to bury him," Jennifer said. "And you owe me a favor."

"He does?" Constance said.

"I do?" Fargo echoed.

Her hand at her side where her sister couldn't see, Jennifer brushed her fingers across Fargo's. "I kept you company when you couldn't sleep, remember?"

"You did what?" Constance said.

"That should count for something," Jennifer said.

"I'll be damned," Fargo said. Here he'd thought she just wanted to make love.

"So will you?" Jennifer asked. "Spare him? Bring him back as your prisoner and not draped over a saddle?"

"I can't make any promises," Fargo said. "He might not give me a choice."

"Oh, Father would never try to hurt *you*," Jennifer said.

"Not in a million years," Constance agreed. "He'd never harm a hair on anyone's head."

Fargo wished he'd brought his bottle. The more he learned, the more the whole situation made no damn sense.

They had passed the Aces High and were halfway along the next block. The boardinghouse was up ahead, and Fargo wondered if Tassy had freed herself.

Marshal Cripdin came out of his office across the street. He went to stretch his arms, saw them, and wheeled and went back in.

"Goodness, did you see the look he gave you?" Constance asked.

"I'm one of his favorite people," Fargo said. He saw the curtains that covered the window to Tassy's room move and wondered if she had seen them. He didn't wonder long.

She came marching out of the boardinghouse and down the porch steps. At the street she turned toward them.

"Here comes that saloon hussy," Jennifer said to her sister.

"Why does she look so mad?" Constance said.

Fargo noticed that Tassy was carrying a handbag, and that her hand was in it. A premonition balled his gut into a knot a heartbeat before she pulled her hand out and raised a pistol.

13

It was a Colt pocket pistol, as they were called, a short-barreled revolver favored by those who used hideouts. Tassy pointed it at him and said, "I'm going to kill you."

Fargo stopped cold. He could draw and shoot her in a twinkling, but he'd rather not.

Jennifer blurted, "What in the world?"

Constance put a hand to her throat. "What do you think you're doing?"

"Stand aside, both of you," Tassy commanded.

Neither girl moved.

"Lower that gun right this instant," Jennifer said.

"If you don't I'll fetch the marshal," Constance warned.

"This doesn't concern you," Tassy said.

"Skye is our friend," Jennifer said. "We won't let you shoot him."

"And I won't let him harm Cord Blasingame," Tassy replied. "I mean it. Both of you step away."

"Are you drunk?" Jennifer said. "You can't go around waving guns at people."

"I'm not waving it," Tassy said. She was growing angrier by the moment. "If you don't move your little asses, it'll be on your heads."

Constance asked, "What is Cord Blasingame to you, anyhow?"

Fargo was aware that other people had stopped to stare and hoped one of them would have the presence of mind to run for the marshal. Cripdin might be next to useless but Tassy might listen if he ordered her to drop the pistol.

"Cord Blasingame is the best man I've ever met," Tassy replied. "He's the one I intend to spend the rest of my days with."

"You're in love with him?" Constance asked in surprise.

"With our—" Jennifer caught herself before she got out "father."

"What if I am?" Tassy said. "It's between him and me and has nothing to do with you."

"That's where you're mistaken," Constance said.

"Connie, don't," Jennifer said.

Tassy was red in the face. The gash where Fargo had hit her with the table was discolored and swollen. "Damn you bitches, anyway."

"We won't be talked to like that," Jennifer said. "Not by a saloon tart, we won't."

"No," Constance said. "And I'll thank you to stop pointing that gun at us." She started toward Tassy.

"Stop, you stupid bitch!" Tassy warned. Her thumb, which was on the pistol's hammer, began to pull the hammer back.

Fargo drew and fired from the hip. He took a gamble and shot at her hand, not at her head or her chest. His countless hours of practice paid off; the slug struck her pistol—even as it went off.

The slug meant for him caught Constance in the middle of her forehead. She staggered, her eyes going wide. Her mouth opened and closed and her body went limp and she slowly collapsed.

Jennifer screamed.

The pocket pistol had been smashed from Tassy's grasp. Cursing, Tassy dived for it. She snatched it up and spun and pointed it at Fargo and pulled back the hammer.

Fargo fanned the Colt twice. This time he didn't hold

back. Both slugs cored her dead center. The impact knocked her onto her back.

Silence gripped Main Street. Not a soul who had witnessed the shootings moved.

Then boots drummed, and Marshal Cripdin was there. "God in heaven!" he exclaimed in horror, and seemed uncertain what to do.

Jennifer darted to Constance and knelt. Wailing her sister's name, she raised Connie's head to her lap, smearing blood over her hands and her dress.

Shouts broke out. People came running from all directions.

Fargo stepped over to Tassy. Her eyes, twin pools of hate, locked on his. "You killed an innocent girl," he said, and felt a twinge of conscience that he hadn't shot sooner.

"Bas . . . tard," Tassy gasped. Blood was oozing from the corners of her mouth. She looked up at the sky, cried out, "Cord!" and died.

Fargo began to replace the spent cartridges. He couldn't bring himself to look at the sisters.

Marshal Cripdin held out his hand. "I'll take that revolver."

"No," Fargo said, "you won't."

"Damn you. I saw you shoot Tassy with my own eyes."

"Did you see her shoot Constance?"

"Yes, but—"

"She did it to protect Cord Blasingame."

"The hell you say."

"You heard her yell."

Cripdin gazed at the body in disbelief. "I knew she was fond of him but I never figured she'd do anything like this."

"How did you know?"

"I beg your pardon?"

"How the hell did you know that Tassy was in love with Blasingame?"

The lawman straightened. "Don't take that tone with me. It was common knowledge, I should think." Flustered, he wheeled. "You men there. We can't have bodies lying in the street. Find blankets to cover these women and we'll carry them to the undertaker's."

A scream pierced the air. The crowd parted for Glenda, who clutched at her chest and stretched out her other hand toward Constance. "No," she said. "No, no, no, no."

Fargo shoved the Colt into his holster. He was going to go to her but Jennifer rose and mother and daughter embraced, both of them crying uncontrollably.

Onlookers were whispering. Several pointed at Fargo. An elderly woman he'd never seen before said, "This is all your fault, mister."

"You should never have come here," a man said.

Fargo wheeled and stalked to the Aces High. There was nothing he could do for Glenda and Jennifer other than hang around and be glared at by everyone else.

The saloon was empty save for the bartender, who was peering over the batwings. "What happened over there? I see two bodies."

"You have good eyes." Fargo pushed on the batwings and the man hastily got out of his way. Going to the bar, he walked around it and along the shelves.

"Hold on, mister," the bartender said. "What do you think you're doing? No one is allowed behind there but me."

Fargo turned and looked at him.

The man shifted his weight from one foot to the other and said, "I reckon it's all right this one time."

Grabbing a bottle, Fargo slapped money, came back around, and walked out. He went up the street to Glenda's, let himself in by the front door, and walked the length of the hall to the kitchen. Taking a seat at the table, he opened the bottle and chugged.

He had half a mind to say to hell with it and leave town. He was a scout. What was he doing, going after a man with a bounty on his head? What was Cord Blasingame to him? Maybe Blasingame had sent men to kill him. Maybe not. Maybe they'd done it on their own, like Tassy.

The thought of her made him wince. He hated to shoot women. He wasn't one of those who put them on a pedestal but it went against his grain.

The way he figured, he'd be doing Glenda a favor if he climbed on the Ovaro and put Meridian behind him. She'd already lost one daughter.

The bottle was a third gone. He raised it to take another swallow and felt a breeze on the back of his neck. He didn't remember the window being open and shifted in his chair.

It wasn't the window.

It was the back door.

The breed filled the doorway, a Spencer level at his waist. "You do as I say, I not kill you."

Fargo hesitated. He could drop the bottle and go for his Colt but not before the man put one or even two slugs into him.

"You hear me, white man?" the breed said.

"I hear you."

"You smart or you stupid?"

"There are days when I wonder," Fargo said. This was one of them.

"My name Niyanatomie. Whites call me Niyan."

"So I've been told," Fargo said. He remembered it was Tassy who told him, and how sweet she had been when they first met.

"My friend want see you. I take you to him. Do like I say, you live. Not do like I say, you die."

"Your friend?" Fargo said, knowing who it was before he asked.

"Cord Blasingame."

"The nicest gent alive," Fargo said, unable to keep the resentment out of his tone.

Niyan tilted his head. "Him good man. Why you sound mad?"

"He's a goddamn outlaw."

"Him good friend," Niyan said. "Him not look down nose because I half red, half white."

"He sent you to bring me?"

Niyan nodded. "Him worried you be killed by others. Three try already."

"Why haven't you tried?"

"Him not want me to," Niyan said, "or you be dead by now."

"Do I get to keep my six-shooter and rifle?"

"Put short gun in saddlebags. Leave long gun in saddle scabbard. I ride behind you. We have far to go. Start now." Niyan paused. "Yes or no?"

Not two minutes ago Fargo had been thinking about leaving. He still wanted to. He could tell the breed he wanted nothing more to do with the whole mess and would like to put Meridian miles behind him, but he doubted the man would let him. Instead he said, "I'd like to meet this boss of yours."

"Cord not boss," Niyan said. "Cord friend." He gestured with the Spencer. "Stand slow. Keep hand from short gun."

"I'm bringing the bottle," Fargo informed him as he rose.

"You have whiskey in blood?"

Fargo knew that was an Indian way of asking if he was a drunk. "I'm taking it to treat your friend Cord to a drink." Blasingame would need one when he heard about his daughter.

"Him like that," Niyan said. "Maybe him and you be friends."

Fargo thought of Constance lying in the street with a bullet hole in her head. "Somehow I doubt it."

14

Fargo had been told the outlaws had a hideout deep in the Shadow Mountains. He reckoned it would take days to reach Blasingame. But barely two hours after riding out of Meridian to the north, Niyan drew rein on the crest of a pine-covered ridge and pointed at smoke rising from a valley. "There him be."

"This close to town?"

"Why not?" Niyan said. "No one try hurt Blasingame. Everyone like him."

"So I keep hearing," Fargo said. "He should run for governor of the territory."

"You like him too. You see."

They wound down the mountain to the valley floor and across to a campfire. Four men were seated around it. Beyond, horses were picketed.

None of the outlaws showed any alarm. None grabbed for a revolver or a rifle. Two were drinking coffee and two others playing cards.

One of the drinkers, who looked as if he hadn't washed his face in a month of Sundays, scowled and said, "So you went and brought him, after all." He had a rifle propped against his leg but wasn't wearing a six-shooter.

"Cord ask me, Nesbit," Niyan said. "I do."

A short man set down his cards, picked up a double-barreled shotgun, and trained it on Fargo. "I still say it's a mistake. I should blow him to kingdom come."

A tall man with a bowie on his hip reached out and pushed the twin muzzles at the ground. "Behave yourself, Hardy."

"Don't tell me what to do, Mills," Hardy growled. "No one ever tells me what to do."

"Does that include me, Hardy?" asked someone in the woods behind them, and out of the trees strolled a broad-shouldered man with curly blond hair and eyes as blue as Fargo's. He was dressed the best of them, in clean clothes, his black boots recently polished. He was also unarmed.

"You're the exception," Hardy replied, reluctantly setting down the shotgun. "You know that, Cord. Hell, you could tell me to jump off a cliff and I would."

Fargo focused on the newcomer. So this was the great Cord Blasingame? Tassy had been right—he was handsome. He also had an easygoing air about him and a genuinely friendly expression.

Blasingame came around the fire and over to the bay and held out his hand to Niyan. "I'm obliged for you bringing him to me. I knew I could count on you."

The breed shook and said sheepishly, "I happy to help, Cord."

"Did he give you any trouble?"

"Him come easy," Niyan said.

Blasingame turned and offered his hand to Fargo. "Thank you. I appreciate you taking the time to see me."

Fargo pumped hands, more mystified than ever. This wasn't the reception he'd imagined. "I don't know what in hell to make of you," he admitted.

Blasingame had a deep laugh. "I can imagine. I'm sorry about Clemens and the others. Climb down and I'll explain and do my best to make things right."

Dismounting, Fargo started to open a saddlebag.

"No," Niyan warned, training the Spencer. "Leave short gun be."

"Short gun?" Hardy exclaimed, and snatched up his shotgun.

Blasingame stepped in front of Fargo, shielding him with his own body. "No shooting. I invited him here. He's under my protection."

Fargo wondered how he could protect anyone when he was unarmed. "I brought a bottle. Are you a drinking man?"

Cord Blasingame had an easy smile. "I do like a nip or three each night. It's one of the many things my wife disliked about me."

"Women," Hardy said, and spat.

Fargo opened the saddlebag and took out the whiskey. He noticed that Niyan covered him, and that Hardy and the one called Nesbit were both poised to shoot.

"Were you surprised by my invitation?" Blasingame asked.

"Since I rode into Meridian," Fargo said, "it's been one surprise after another."

"Imagine my own when I was told you're staying with my wife and those darling girls of mine."

Fargo opened the bottle and swigged. He wiped it with his sleeve and held it out to the outlaw leader. "Help yourself."

"I thank you, kindly." Blasingame drank and let out an "Ahhh. Monongahela is my favorite coffin varnish."

"I like rum," Nesbit said. "My pa was a sailor and it's all he ever had in the house."

Blasingame passed the bottle back. "I should introduce my friends. You've already met Niyan. These others are"— and he pointed at each of them in turn—"Hardy, with the shotgun, Nesbit, who could use a bath, and Mills, wearing the bowie. That last there is Davies. He can't talk. He was thrown by a pony when he was ten and it kicked him in the throat."

Davies nodded at Fargo. He was large and sullen and dressed all in gray and had a Starr revolver on his left hip.

"There were three more of us," Blasingame said, "but you went and killed them."

"You're taking it awful well," Fargo remarked.

"They were friends," Blasingame said, "but they went against my wishes." He stopped. "Well, Zeke and Barnes did. When they heard you were after me, there was no stopping them."

"And Clemens?"

"I was told he overheard my wife talking about how she'd sent for you. He took it on himself to camp out at the pass."

"Overheard her?" Fargo said.

"My men keep an eye on my family for me," Blasingame said. "I like to keep track of the girls. Any father worth a damn would." He sat and patted the ground. "Make yourself comfortable."

The man was being so friendly, it made Fargo suspicious. Sitting, he drank more whiskey and passed the bottle to Blasingame, who took a sip and passed it back.

"It's early yet," he said. "Too much at this time of day gives me a headache."

"It doesn't give me one," Mills said, "but no one's offered me a drink." He glared at Fargo.

"Pass it around," Fargo said. The more they drank, the more it would slow their reflexes.

"Now then," Blasingame said. "You must be wondering why I sent for you."

"I figured it wasn't to pass the time of day," Fargo said.

"I understand my wife has offered to split the bounty with you whether you bring me in dead or alive."

"Is there anything she does you don't know?"

Blasingame laughed. "She leaves windows cracked open to let in air. Always did that back in Saint Louis, too. Makes it easy to spy on her."

"You still care for her after all this time?"

"Not in the way you mean, no." Blasingame grew thoughtful. "I loved Glenda once. I married her, after all.

And she gave us two fine daughters. It's them I love more than anything in this world."

Fargo dreaded the moment that was coming.

"But now the best I can say is that I consider her something of a friend even though she doesn't feel the same about me." Blasingame motioned. "You're proof of that. If she still cared, she wouldn't have sent for you."

"If it hadn't been me," Fargo mentioned, "it would have been someone else."

"True. She hates me, I'm afraid. Hates me with every fiber of her being for leaving her. Hates me so much that when she found out where I was, she came here hoping to bury me."

"You walked out on them."

Blasingame reacted as if Fargo had punched him. Stricken, he bowed his head. "I just couldn't take it anymore," he said in a small voice. "Couldn't take her. You have no idea what she's like."

"I'm all ears," Fargo said. Actually, he was stalling so the outlaws could finish the bottle, and he could put off saying what he had to.

"Glenda is a bitch, Skye," Blasingame said. "Nothing I did was ever good enough for her. Morning to night, she carped. She criticized. She pointed out my failings. Year after year this went on until finally I had to get out of there before I did something I'd regret."

"And your girls?"

The pain on Blasingame's face deepened. "God, I hated leaving them. But they were almost grown. I figured it was better that they be mad at me for leaving than be mad at me for caving Glenda's skull in with a hammer." He quickly added, "Not that I would. I've never harmed another human being my whole life."

Fargo studied him. "You're an *outlaw*. How's that possible?"

It was Hardy who answered. "Any killin' he needs done, the rest of us do it."

"Gladly," Mills said.

Nesbit nodded.

Davies too.

Niyan sat as stone-faced as an Apache but his dark eyes glittered.

"That they do, I'm afraid," Blasingame said.

"I'll be damned." Fargo looked at him and then at each of the others, and shook his head. "It still doesn't make much sense."

"Sure it does, mister," Hardy said. "Cord's the brains and we're the bullets."

"Or the knife," Mills said, and patted his bowie.

"Cord's the one came up with the idea how and when to rob the bank," Hardy said. "And it's him as picks the stages and where to stop them so there's less chance of anyone bein' hurt."

"Less chance?" Fargo said.

"Of course," Blasingame said. "I'm not in this to hurt people. Only to get enough money for them"—and he nodded at the others—"so they don't have to be outlaws anymore."

"What?" Fargo said.

"That's right," Hardy said. "Once each of us has ten thousand dollars we're goin' our separate ways and changin' our names and startin' over."

"A whole new lease on life, is how Cord puts it," Mills said.

"I aim to buy me a pig farm and settle down and live high on the hog," Nesbit said.

Just when Fargo thought he'd heard everything.

"And now you come along," Hardy said, "and threaten to spoil everything."

"We don't like that," Mills said.

"Not like at all," Niyan broke his long silence, and raised his Spencer.

15

"Put that down," Cord Blasingame said, holding his hand over the muzzle. "Unless you're willing to blow my fingers off."

Scowling, Niyan obeyed. "I happy if we kill him so him not kill you."

"You would be but I wouldn't," Blasingame said, and faced Fargo. "Which is why I have a proposition for you."

"For me?" Fargo said. The bottle, he noticed, was almost gone. Davies had drunk the least, Hardy and Mills the most.

"We always split our earnings fairly," Blasingame said. "Equal shares for everyone so we—"

"You don't earn it," Fargo said. "You steal it."

"Well, yes, there's that. My point, though, is that I have about four thousand dollars hid away. It's yours, every penny, if you'll mount up and ride off and forget about the bounty."

"You're serious?"

"I know what you're thinking," Blasingame said. "Half the bounty is five thousand. So you'd lose about a thousand in the bargain. But you wouldn't have to kill me to get it, and none of my men will kill you to stop you."

"Sounds fair to me," Mills said.

"More than fair," Hardy growled. "If it was me, I'd blow his damn head off."

"Now, now," Blasingame said. "You agreed to let me handle this."

"I don't like it," Hardy said. "Him huntin' you down like you're a damn animal."

"He hasn't had to do any hunting," Blasingame said. "And if he accepts my offer, all your worry is for nothing."

"You're splittin' hairs," Hardy said. "Anyone who'd hunt a man for money is as low as low can be."

"How many men have you killed?" Fargo asked.

"That's different."

"Hardy, please," Blasingame said. "You're not helping matters." He smiled at Fargo. "What do you say? Make it easy on all of us. And safer for Glenda and my daughters. I heard about Barnes trying to kill you in their house."

Fargo had put it off long enough. The smart thing to do, he supposed, was to keep his mouth shut, but the man deserved to know. "About them," he said.

"Who?"

"Tassy tried to stop me from coming after you."

Blasingame stiffened. "She did what?"

"She came after me with a pistol." Fargo hated to say it, and took a deep breath. "She shot Connie in the head by mistake. And I shot her."

The outlaws froze.

"Constance is dead?" Blasingame said, incredulous. "Tassy too?"

"I'm sorry," Fargo said, and meant it.

It was Hardy who recovered from the shock first. "You son of a bitch!" he snarled, and grabbed his shotgun.

Mills started to draw his bowie.

Davies put a hand on his revolver.

"No!" Blasingame shouted. "You gave your word!" A tear had formed in the corner of his eye, and it trickled down his cheek to his chin.

The other outlaws watched it as if fascinated.

"My sweet, wonderful Connie," Blasingame said, and his body shook. "God, no."

"Tassy was in love with you, wasn't she?" Fargo needed to have it clear.

Numbly, Blasingame nodded. "I've been seeing her for a while now. She planned to go with me once I have enough to start over. I never imagined—" He stopped. "And she shot Connie by mistake, you say?"

"There were witnesses."

"Son of a bitch," Hardy said. "Son of a bitch, son of a bitch, son of a bitch."

"I liked both those gals," Mills said.

"What about Jennifer?" Blasingame asked.

"She's fine," Fargo said. Or as fine as someone could be after seeing their sister's brains blown out.

"I have to go to her," Blasingame said, abruptly rising. "And to Glenda."

"It's not safe," Mills said.

"You can come with me if you're worried," Blasingame said. "The rest of you will stay here with Fargo."

"I'm coming too," Fargo said.

Blasingame shook his head. "I'd rather you didn't. We haven't finished our talk yet."

"It's not up to you."

Niyan pointed the Spencer. "Him say you stay, you stay."

"You're not goin' anywhere, mister," Hardy said, cradling the shotgun.

Nesbit nodded.

"I'm sorry," Blasingame said. "This is how it has to be." He beckoned to Mills and together they hurried to the horse string, climbed on their animals, and departed at a gallop.

In the silence that fell Fargo glanced at his saddlebags and the saddle scabbard. His Colt and Henry might as well be on the moon.

"Make yourself comfortable," Hardy said. "It'll be a while before he gets back."

"We can play cards," Nesbit said. "Have any money you can bet?"

"A little," Fargo said. It would keep them busy, and distract them, and maybe give him a chance to get to his guns.

Nesbit picked up the cards and shuffled. "I'll deal. Jacks or better to open."

Fargo was quick to notice that one of them wasn't given any cards. "What about Niyan?"

"I never play," the breed said. "Stupid to lose money."

"That's Injun logic for you," Hardy said, and laughed.

"This half-Injun have more money than you," Niyan said. "You lose much."

"I'll win it back," Hardy boasted. "And more besides."

Fargo played poorly. His mind wasn't on the game. It was on Cord Blasingame, who was bound to hear that it was his shot that spoiled Tassy's aim and caused her to shoot Constance. Blasingame might blame him, in part, for her death. How friendly would he be then? He'd rather not stay there and find out.

"Hey, mister," Hardy said. "Pay attention. It's your bet. Are you in or are you out?"

Fargo folded so he could think. He had to get out of there. Stretching, he remarked, "That whiskey went right through me. I need to piss."

"I go with you," Niyan said.

"You fixing to hold my pecker for me too?" Fargo said as he stood and started toward the forest.

"Let him go," Hardy said to the breed. "He's not goin' anywhere without his horse."

Fargo inwardly smiled. He went a few yards into the trees and stopped.

Hardy, Nesbit and Davies had gone on playing cards. Niyan was staring at the woods.

Fargo moved quickly. If he took too long, they'd wonder. The Ovaro was where he'd left it when he dismounted, the reins dangling. To reach it he either had to go past the outlaws or do what he now did, namely, crouch and stalk from cover keeping the horse string between him and the outlaws. The horses ignored him; they were used to his scent by now. Moving along the string to the end, he edged around the last horse.

Niyan was still staring at the spot where he'd entered the forest. The rest were betting on their hands.

Fargo coiled his legs. All he needed was for the breed to look away. If he broke into the open now, Niyan would see him.

"I see your raise, Hardy," Nesbit was saying. "I think you're bluffin'."

"Sometimes I do and sometimes I don't," Hardy said with a smirk, "and this is one of those I'm not." He showed his cards with a flourish. "A full house, by God. Kings and twos."

"Damn it to hell," Nesbit said, and threw down his hand in disgust. "I don't know why I bother. I always lose more than I win."

Hardy raked in the coins and bills, then glanced toward the forest. "What's takin' that hombre so long? He could have peed a river by now."

"Say, you're right," Nesbit said.

"Davies, go have a look-see."

The silent man went to rise but Niyan stood first. "I go," the breed said.

"It could be a trick of his. Be careful he doesn't jump you," Hardy cautioned.

"I not you," Niyan replied. "I not careless."

Nesbit laughed and slapped his leg. "He's got you there, Hardy."

Here was Fargo's chance. Two of the outlaws had their backs to him. Davies was facing in his direction but was busy gathering up cards since it was his turn to deal.

The moment the undergrowth swallowed Niyan, Fargo broke into motion. He was almost to the Ovaro when a yell came from the trees.

"Him go for horse!"

Fargo snatched the reins on the fly. Grabbing the saddle horn, he forked his leg up and over. A jab of his spurs and he was at a gallop.

"Stop him!" Hardy bawled.

Fargo went twenty yards before a shot boomed, and it was a rifle, not the shotgun. He heard the buzz of lead past his ear and began zigzagging.

A look back showed Hardy, Nesbit and Davies scrambling for their picketed mounts. It also showed Niyan bounding toward his bay.

Fargo wanted his Colt but it would have to wait. He concentrated on riding, on putting distance between him and his pursuers. When no more shots rang out he flew straight across the valley floor and had a good lead when he reached the timbered slope. He didn't stop until he'd climbed to the crest.

The outlaws were hard after him, Niyan well out in front.

Fargo reined down the other side of the mountain. If he could somehow shake Niyan he'd be in the clear. The others were too far behind to catch him.

He kept glancing back, concerned the breed would try to pick him off. Along about the eighth or ninth time, he looked and then faced front—only to see a limb directly in his path. It was too low for him to duck.

Fargo tried to swerve but in the fraction of time it took him to pull on the reins, the limb struck him across the chest with brutal force.

The impact swept him from the saddle and his world exploded in pain.

16

Fargo didn't feel his body crash to the ground. The pain eclipsed nearly every other sensation. He was vaguely aware the stallion had kept on going and knew it wouldn't go far.

Struggling not to pass out, he got his hands under him, and rolled over. The effort brought a fresh wave of agony. He sensed that nothing was broken although he couldn't be sure.

His vision swimming, he rolled a second time and felt leaves brush his face. Hooves pounded, and for a few harrowing moments he thought Niyan would ride right over him. But the hooves drummed past.

Suddenly he could see again. He was in a thicket. The impact had knocked him not only clear of his saddle but sent him flying a good eight to ten feet. Smothering a groan, he sat up.

He looked to the right and saw the other outlaws fifty to sixty yards away, coming on fast. He looked to the left and there was Niyan, about to overtake the Ovaro, which had slowed. The breed was glancing all around.

Fargo flattened and crawled. His Colt was still in his saddlebag and the Henry in the scabbard. All he had on him was the toothpick and it was no match for revolvers and rifles.

The pain subsided a little. He moved faster and crawled under a spruce.

A shout from Hardy heralded the arrival of the other three.

"Where is he?"

Niyan was returning, leading the Ovaro by the reins. "Here horse."

"I can see that, dammit," Hardy said. "Where the hell is *he*?"

"Him jump or maybe hit limb."

"You didn't see?"

"Lose sight of him for bit," Niyan said, "then see him not on horse."

"Great, just great," Hardy spat, and swore. "Spread out, all of you! He can't have gone far."

"What do we do when we find him?" Nesbit asked. "Cord said we're not to harm him."

"Cord ain't here," Hardy said.

"I don't like goin' against Cord."

"It's for his own good," Hardy said. "What makes me wonder is why Fargo ran like that. We were treatin' him nice."

"Maybe he thought we were goin' to kill him," Nesbit said.

"Just because we're outlaws don't mean our word's no good," Hardy said.

"I'll ask again," Nesbit said, "what do we do when we find him?"

"Truss him up and let Cord decide what to do with him," Hardy said. "Now fan out! And give a holler if you spot the son of a bitch."

The undergrowth crackled to the passage of their horses.

Fargo resumed crawling, circling wide. He spotted Hardy and Nesbit and Davies but didn't see the breed. That bothered him. Then he spied the bay standing next to the Ovaro.

Niyan had climbed down to search on foot. Which made him doubly dangerous.

The nearest rider was Nesbit. He kept rising in the stirrups and looking all around and sinking down again.

Fargo froze every time Nesbit looked in his direction.

Hardy was to the east.

Davies had gone to the north.

Fargo still couldn't spot Niyan. Scrabbling like a giant lizard, he continued to circle.

Nesbit passed within twenty feet and went on to the south.

A little farther, and Fargo was close to the Ovaro and the bay. He was about to make a run for the stallion when he froze.

Moccasins had appeared about ten feet to his left. It was Niyan, in a crouch, stalking in his direction. The breed must have heard him even though he had been moving as quietly as he could.

Fargo inched his hand to his boot. He wouldn't let them recapture him. So what if they were only going to tie him? Once Blasingame heard about Constance, the outlaw leader might well want him dead.

Niyan made no noise whatsoever. He was studying every shadow, every possible hiding place.

Fargo gripped the hilt of the Arkansas toothpick, and tensed. The instant the breed set eyes on him, he'd rush him.

To the northwest a twig cracked.

Niyan whipped around and was off like a shot.

Fargo didn't know what made the twig break. A deer maybe. Fate had smiled on him. The second Niyan was out of sight he was on his feet and running. His chest hurt but he didn't let it slow him. He reached the stallion, snagged the reins, and vaulted into the saddle. He was going to grab the bay's reins too but to the east Hardy gave a shout.

"There he is! He's on his horse!"

Fargo reined to the southwest and rode like hell. Hardy's shotgun boomed but apparently it was a warning shot; the buckshot hit limbs well above him.

Hugging the saddle horn, Fargo lashed his reins. He put all his skill to the test. The crash of growth told him they were after him but he didn't look back. He wouldn't make the same mistake twice.

Gradually the sounds of pursuit faded. He slowed to a trot and went another quarter-mile and finally drew rein to give the Ovaro a breather.

As he waited, he pondered.

Things had gone to hell. Constance was dead. Tassy had given her life trying to protect the man she loved. The local law wouldn't mind if he, too, ended up in an early grave. Practically the whole town was against him. Ironically, the ones who treated him the best were the outlaws. And their leader had turned out to be the most well-liked gent in the territory, and easy to get along with.

Fargo made up his mind. This bounty business wasn't for him. He'd let Glenda know that he was bowing out and light a shuck. He should stick to what he knew.

The sun was down when he reached Meridian. Lights glowed in windows and a few horses were at hitch rails but otherwise signs of life were few. The marshal's office was dark.

Fargo was tempted to stop at the Aces High but didn't. He went up the path to the front door of the house Glenda was renting, and knocked. When no one came he knocked louder.

Someone mumbled something. Feet shuffled and the door opened.

Glenda Blasingame was a pitiful sight. Tears streaked her face and her hair was disheveled. Her dress had a tear. She sniffled and blinked and then seemed to realize who it was. "Skye!" she cried, and to his surprise, she threw herself at him and embraced him as if he were a long-lost relative. "Oh, Skye. You came back."

Fargo tried to disentangle her but she clung fast and sobbed into his neck. "What the hell?"

"Oh, Skye," she said again, and sagged.

Scooping her into his arms, Fargo stepped inside, kicked the door shut, and carried her to the parlor. He carefully set her on the settee. The whole time, she wept and shook.

Fargo figured she was still crying over Constance. Patting her hand, he said, "I'll get you a drink." A glass of whiskey might help calm her.

"No," Glenda said, and grabbed his hand in both of hers. "I don't need that. I need you to go after them."

"After who?" Fargo said. "Your husband? That's what I came to talk to you about. I'm through."

"You can't be!" Glenda cried, and with fierce strength she pulled him down beside her. "You're my only hope. I can't count on Cripdin."

"Glenda, listen—" Fargo began.

"Hear me out, please," she begged. "Losing Connie was almost more than I could bear. I can't lose her, too."

"Lose who?"

"Jennifer. Who else?" Glenda sniffled and wiped her nose with her sleeve. "He took her, Skye. The bastard marched in here and stole her away. Him and that Mills."

"Cord took Jennifer?"

Glenda nodded. "He'd stopped at the saloon and heard about Connie and that Tassy. He said it was all my fault. That if I hadn't sent for you, they'd both still be alive." She uttered another sob. "He said I wasn't fit to be their mother. And that he'd be damned if he'd stand by and let Jennifer be hurt, or worse. So he took her."

"Did she want to go with him?"

"Of course not," Glenda exploded. "She refused and tried to fight but Mills got her hands behind her back and tied her. I couldn't do a thing. Cord had hold of me and wouldn't let go."

"Damn," Fargo said.

"As soon as they left I ran to the marshal's office. Cripdin is off with a posse trying to find her but we both know he won't." Glenda clutched at his buckskin shirt. "You're

97

my only hope. You have to go after them. You have to bring my girl back."

The hell of it was, Fargo agreed. He felt he owed it to Jennifer after the other night. "I'll leave at first light."

"Why not now?"

"I can't track in the dark," Fargo replied, "and my horse needs the rest."

"Oh God." Glenda pressed her forehead to his chest and closed her eyes. "I shudder to think of her spending the night with those killers and robbers."

"Your husband won't let anything happen to her."

"My *former* husband," Glenda said bitterly. "May he rot in hell."

Fargo shared her sentiment but for a whole different reason. He'd looked forward to being shed of this mess; now he was being drawn back in.

"I pleaded with him not to take her but he refused to listen."

"Maybe you shouldn't talk about it."

Glenda acted as if she hadn't heard. "I told him that if he was going to assign blame, he should point a finger at himself. He's the one who dallied with that saloon tart. If he'd stayed true to me it never would have happened."

"How about some coffee?"

"What I want," Glenda said, "is my daughter safe and my husband dead. Show him no mercy. When you find them, shoot him, stab him, cave in his skull with a rock. I don't care. Kill him any way you can and make me the happiest woman alive."

17

Fargo ate a light supper. As much as he wouldn't mind some coffin varnish and a game of poker, he turned in early. He stripped off his shirt and boots and stretched out with his hands behind his head. He drifted off easily enough and might have slept the night through if not for the creak of a door hinge.

Fargo awoke with a start. He listened, heard a soft rustle, and started to reach for his gun belt, which he'd placed near his pillow.

"Skye?"

Perfume wreathed him and Glenda sat on the edge of the bed.

"I couldn't sleep. I'm too worried about Jennifer."

"Your husband will take good care of her," Fargo said. Whatever else Cord Blasingame might be, he was devoted to his daughters.

"I wish you'd quit calling him that. He stopped being my husband the day he abandoned me." Glenda paused. "Would you mind some company?"

Fargo misconstrued and said, "I don't feel like talking right now."

"Neither do I." Glenda stood and pulled back the blanket. "I don't want to be alone. Please. All I want is to get some sleep."

"It's your house," Fargo said, "your bed."

"Thank you."

Sliding in, Glenda lay on her back and primly pulled the blanket to her chin. "I won't be a bother."

Fargo grunted and rolled over on his side with his back to her. That should convince her he really did want to sleep. But no sooner did he do so than a hand fell on his shoulder.

"I appreciate this."

Fargo was getting good at grunting.

"I want to sleep but I'm too overwrought. I don't know as I can without help."

"Help how?"

Her hand moved to his arm and gently squeezed. "I was thinking we could—" She stopped. "That is, if you're not too tired."

Fargo was never too tired for *that*. But with one daughter dead and the other taken, he wouldn't have thought she'd be in the mood.

"I know what you're thinking," Glenda said. "I guess I had no right to call Tassy a tart when I'm not much better."

Fargo rolled onto his back. She immediately shifted and lightly caressed his arm and his side.

"Like that?" she asked.

"I'd have to be a damn fool not to."

"So would you like to or not? Don't keep me in suspense."

Fargo kissed her. She responded passionately, her tongue entwining with his. He cupped a breast and felt her nipple harden. He felt a growing hunger, but at the back of his mind a tiny voice warned that something wasn't right.

Evidently Glenda sensed his reserve. Pulling back, she asked, "Is something the matter?"

"Only that you talk too much." Fargo squeezed harder. He decided to hell with it. If she wanted a poke, he'd be happy to oblige. Whatever she was up to would come out eventually.

Her cotton robe was belted at the waist. A tug, and it parted and fell away. Her tits were twice again as big as Jennifer's but her nipples were smaller. He pinched and tweaked and she squirmed and cooed.

"God, I want you," she husked in his ear.

Lowering his mouth to a breast, Fargo nipped and licked and rimmed the tip with his tongue. She arched her back and dug her fingernails into his shoulders.

After a while he dipped lower. Panting with every breath, she cried out at the contact.

Fargo lost track of the time. He had been sleepy but now he wasn't. He kissed and fondled and was treated in turn, and then he was on his knees between her outspread thighs, about to mount her.

"Yes," Glenda breathed. "Oh, yes." Reaching for him, she guided him in, and when their bodies were flush, she sank her teeth into his arm.

The bed bounced fit to bust. Downstairs, the clock chimed three.

Holding her hips, Fargo let himself go. She wanted it; he'd give it to her. He thrust so powerfully, he lifted both of them off the bed.

Glenda reached the summit first. Throwing back her head, she let out a scream. As she subsided, she realized he hadn't exploded. "What are you—" she said, and got no further.

Fargo erupted. He rammed fit to cleave her in two. He felt her sheath contract, milking him, and she tossed her head from side to side as she gushed anew.

Afterward, covered with sweat, he lay on his side listening to her breathe and wondering what that had been about.

Sleep crept up on him and sucked him under. He might have slept past first light if not for her elbow poking him when she rolled over. He opened his eyes and had to fight to keep them open. His arms and legs leaden, he sat up and yawned and stretched.

Glenda let out a snore, her robe crumpled under her, fanny bare to the world.

Fargo smacked her backside hard enough to leave a handprint.

Screeching, Glenda pushed up onto her elbows and looked around in confusion. "What the hell?" she blurted. She saw him and frowned. "Oh. It's only you."

"I love you too," Fargo said.

"Don't ever say that, not even in jest," Glenda angrily scolded. She slid her legs over the side of the bed and shrugged into her robe. "You didn't have to wake me that way."

"Someone is a bitch in the morning."

Glancing sharply over her shoulder, Glenda snapped, "I'll thank you to be more civil." She stood. "I deserve it after last night, don't you think?"

"You deserve this," Fargo said, and gave her another smack on the rump. He didn't hold back.

Glenda yelped and jumped and rubbed herself. "Damn you. Stop that!"

"You want me to stop," Fargo said, "make us some coffee."

"All you had to do was ask."

Fargo filled the china bowl with water from the pitcher and washed up. He took his time dressing and tugging into his boots. He jammed his hat on, strapped the Colt around his waist, and ambled downstairs.

The kitchen was fragrant with the scent of brewing coffee, and more.

Glenda bustled about, going from the stove to the counter to the table. "Breakfast will be ready in a few minutes. I didn't want you to go off hungry."

Fargo hadn't asked for food but the sight of scrambled eggs and frying bacon made his stomach growl. Pulling out a chair, he sat. "You're a fine cook," he said for want of anything else.

"You'll need your strength going after Cord and those animals who ride with him." Glenda looked up from the toast she was buttering. "Play it safe and kill them all. If you don't, the others will come after you for shooting him."

"You're taking it for granted I will."

Glenda stopped buttering. "Why wouldn't you? The bounty is for dead or alive. Why make it harder on yourself than it has to be?"

"Dead *or* alive," Fargo said. "I get to decide."

"How can you even think of alive after all he's done? He deserted me and the girls. He became an outlaw, for God's sake. Now he's abducted Jennifer."

"His daughter."

"And your friend, or so I thought," Glenda said. "Or don't you care what happens to her?"

"Knowing him," Fargo said, "he hasn't done anything to harm her."

Glenda wagged the butter knife at him. "Don't tell me he's fooled you too."

"Fooled me how?"

"That act he puts on. Of being friendly. Of wrapping people around his finger and having them fall over themselves to do things for him."

It hadn't seemed like an act to Fargo, and he mentioned as much.

"Then you're as gullible as everyone else. He did it to me when we were married and I admit I didn't see through him until near the very end."

Fargo wondered; could she be right? Was Cord using people? Politicians did it all the time. They cozied up to folks to get their votes. Drummers and clerks and patent medicine men did it to get people to buy what they were selling.

"I expected better of you," Glenda was saying. "I thought you were sharper."

"Don't make more of me than there is."

"There's no excuse for being taken in when you know the truth." Glenda turned to the counter, and the toast. "I've said enough. I leave his fate in your hands. See him for what he is and not what he pretends to be and you'll agree with me. Cord has to die."

After that somber note they didn't say another word the whole course of the meal.

Fargo ate heartily. Six eggs, thick bacon strips, two slices of toast and five cups of coffee. He would have eaten more except it would make him sluggish. Pushing back his plate, he said, "That husband of yours was a jackass to leave you."

Glenda brightened. "What a sweet thing to say. I'll tell you what. I'll pack some food for you to take along and you can be on your way."

It took only a few minutes. She followed him out to the Ovaro and stood with her arms folded while he put the food in his saddlebags.

"Be careful, will you?"

"Goes without saying," Fargo said.

"He's slick, Cord is," Glenda said. "He smiles and acts nice and you think he's the greatest gent alive. But it's how he manipulates people. How he bends them to his will."

"You told me all that inside."

"I know. I just need you to realize the truth. You can't bring my Jennifer back if you're dead, and she's all I have left in this world."

Fargo hooked his boot in the stirrup and swung up. The saddle creaked under him, and he lifted the reins. "I can promise you this. If he or any of his men have hurt Jennifer, I'll hunt the bastards down and bury them."

Glenda smiled happily. "That's more like it."

Fargo gigged the Ovaro and rode around the house to

the main street. The few people abroad all stared. Word about him had spread and everyone knew who he was.

He'd meant what he said about the outlaws and Jennifer. If they'd hurt the girl, a lot more blood would be spilled before this was done.

18

They were wily bastards.

Or, rather, Niyan was.

Fargo returned to where the outlaws had been camped when he made his break for freedom. Tracks showed that three riders had come from the direction of town—Cord Blasingame, Jennifer and Mills, he figured—and the whole bunch had gone off to the north. Given how many horses were involved, it should have been easy to track them.

It wasn't.

Early on, Fargo noticed that they stuck to rocky ground where there was any and the hardest ground where there wasn't much rock. When they passed through forest they avoided slopes where oaks and other leafy trees grew in abundance and instead favored stretches of pine and spruce. The reason was obvious; the thick cushion of pine needles left few signs.

Niyan's doing, Fargo reckoned, since an unshod horse was in the lead, and Indians, and those of half-blood, almost always rode horses without shoes.

Whenever the outlaws came to a stream, they'd ride in the middle for a mile or two. A trick that would throw green trackers off their scent but Fargo wasn't green. He knew that unless a stream was especially swift-flowing, hooves sank so deep that the tracks weren't always washed away.

Still, it slowed him.

On his third day out of Meridian he was surprised to come across fresh tracks. Not of the outlaws, but of seven other riders, all on shod horses. The seven had crossed the sign left by the outlaws and not realized it. He had a hunch who they were, and on an impulse he reined after them.

About half an hour later, along about noon, he spied smoke. The seven had camped and put coffee on.

Fargo approached at a walk with his hand on his Colt. He wasn't sure of the reception he'd get. He didn't hail them. He simply rode on in.

A townsman in a bowler was the first to spot him and jump to his feet, crying, "Someone is coming!"

The rest all stood, several brandishing rifles.

Marshal Theodore Cripdin hooked his thumbs in his gun belt and said, "Well, look who it is."

Fargo drew rein, and nodded. "Still after them, I see."

"We've crisscrossed these mountains for days now and not come across hide nor hair of the outlaws and that poor girl," Cripdin said.

Fargo gestured at the coffeepot. "Mind if I join you?"

"Suit yourself," the lawman said.

Alighting, Fargo fished his tin cup from his saddlebag and stepped to the fire. The townsmen backed away as if afraid of catching a disease. Hunkering, he remarked to Cripdin, "They seem a mite skittish."

"You've killed three men and one woman since you came to town," the marshal replied. "What the hell do you expect?"

"It was them or me," Fargo said.

"I know. Witnesses told me that Tassy tried to shoot you. Otherwise, I'd have you behind bars. No matter how tough an hombre you think you are."

Fargo let the insult go. He filled his cup and held it in both hands. "There's something you don't know that you should."

"I'm listening."

"Glenda Hemmings. Her real name is Glenda Blasingame. Jennifer is Cord Blasingame's daughter."

The marshal's mouth fell. "The hell you say. You know this for a fact?"

"Glenda sent for me to hunt him down and told me the whole story."

"Well, hell," the townsman wearing the bowler declared. "This changes everything."

Another man bobbed his chin. "Sure does. If she's Blasingame's girl, why are we after them?"

"For all we know," said a third, "she went along willingly."

Marshal Cripdin motioned. "Hold on, all of you. Let's think this out."

"What is there to think about?" the man in the bowler retorted. "Blasingame didn't steal her like we thought. She's his own flesh and blood."

"He has every right to be with her, outlaw or no," another posse member said.

"What are you saying, Floyd?" Cripdin said.

"We should turn back," Floyd responded, and several others bobbed their chins in agreement. "She's not in any danger from her own pa."

Cripdin gnawed his lip, then said, "Let's not jump to any hasty conclusions. I need to ask our friend here a few questions." He turned to Fargo. "You just told us that Glenda hired you. For the bounty?"

"She wants to split it," Fargo said.

"Then how do we know this isn't a trick on your part?"

"Mine?" Fargo said.

"A trick how?" Floyd asked.

"Simple," Cripdin said. "He wants the bounty. To earn it, he has to bring in Blasingame or Blasingame's body himself. But if we find Blasingame, he doesn't get a cent."

"I see what you're saying," Floyd said. "He tricks us into heading back by telling us a tall tale about the girl being Blasingame's kin, and he has Blasingame to himself."

"That's my guess," Cripdin said.

Fargo didn't know whether to laugh in their faces or curse them for being idiots. "Here I reckoned I was doing you a favor."

"That's what made me suspicious," Cripdin said. "You being so nice."

"Ask Glenda," Fargo said.

The marshal grinned. "You'd like that, since we'd have to go all the way back to town."

"How dumb do you think we are, mister?" the man in the bowler asked.

"Pretty damn dumb," Fargo said.

"All right," Cripdin said. "Cover this son of a bitch, boys."

In the blink of an eye, four rifles were leveled. Fargo calmly took a sip while fuming inside.

"We're taking you with us," Cripdin announced. "We have enough grub for two or three days yet, and we're not giving up."

"You don't want to do this," Fargo said.

"Like hell. I've been looking for an excuse and now you've given it to me."

A rifle barrel gouged the back of Fargo's head, and Marshal Cripdin stepped up and relieved him of the Colt.

They didn't bind him.

When they were ready to ride out, they commanded he get on the Ovaro and covered him as he did.

Marshal Cripdin was in fine spirits. "Yes, sir," he said as he brought his sorrel alongside the stallion. "Wait until folks in Meridian hear about this."

"Which way?" Floyd asked.

"How about if we try north?" Cripdin said.

"Deeper into the mountains?" a stocky man wearing a vest brought up.

"They have to be somewhere," Cripdin said.

Fargo could have pointed out that venturing farther in was the worst mistake they could make, that they didn't stand a prayer if the outlaws got wind of them. But he didn't.

All that afternoon the posse pushed on. They weren't in any hurry so by sundown they'd barely covered five miles.

The lawman called a halt on a bench that offered a sweeping view of the Shadow Mountains. He had two men watch Fargo while others saw to the horses and Floyd gathered firewood.

Fargo let them think they had the upper hand. He didn't once act up. When he was told to do something, he did it.

Soon a fire crackled and the man in the brown vest put beans on to cook.

Stars blossomed. A wolf howled and was answered by another.

No one said much until a man remarked, "I wish I was back in town having my nightly drink at the saloon."

"I never thought I'd say this," another piped up, "but I miss my missus."

The man in the vest stirred the pot and said, "Supper should be ready in a bit."

"I am so tired of beans I could vomit," Floyd said. "The first deer we see, we should shoot it and have venison."

"I'm surprised we haven't come across any by now," a man said.

Fargo wasn't. They made enough noise to scare off all the game around. Just one of their many mistakes. Like that fire, he reflected; it was bigger than it should be.

"You're awful quiet," Marshal Cripdin said to him. "Cat got your tongue?"

"Stupid does," Fargo said.

"Do you mean us?"

"You're where you shouldn't be, doing what you shouldn't be doing."

"You're just mad because we got the drop on you. When we get back to town I'm sending you on your way. We'll escort you to Bald Mountain Pass, and if you ever show your face in Meridian again, I'll throw you behind bars and toss away the key." Cripdin sat straighter and squared his plump shoulders, preening for his audience.

"That fire can be seen for miles," Fargo felt compelled to mention.

"All fires can," Cripdin said.

"You wouldn't see an Apache fire unless you were right on top of it."

Floyd laughed. "So what? There ain't any Apaches in these parts. Hell, we haven't seen an Injun of any kind this whole while."

"You're trying to scare us but it won't work," the man in the bowler said.

Fargo was watching the horses and saw the Ovaro raise its head. So did a few others. "Any chance I could have my Colt back?"

Cripdin glanced at his waist. The Colt was tucked under his belt next to his holster. "Not a chance in hell. Why would you even ask?"

"I'm the only one here who stands half a chance," Fargo said.

"I swear," Cripdin said. "You talk more nonsense than anyone I've ever met. Stand a chance against who?"

Just then Hardy strolled into the firelight with his sawed-off shotgun at his hip.

At the same instant, Niyan materialized on the other side of the posse with his Spencer to his shoulder.

"That would be us," Hardy said with a broad grin.

19

Everyone froze except the man called Floyd. "The out-laws!" he shouted, and pushed to his feet, clawing for a revolver on his hip.

Hardy shot him. He shifted the shotgun and let loose with one of the barrels. There was a saying on the frontier that buckshot meant burying, and in this case it did; the hand cannon blew the top of Floyd's head off.

One of the other townsmen screamed and several threw themselves to the ground.

Hardy broke the shotgun open, ejected the spent shell, and inserted another. "Anyone else hankerin' to die?"

"God in heaven!" Marshal Cripdin exclaimed, staring aghast at the oozing cavity in Floyd's skull. "You killed that man."

"I sure as hell did." Snapping the shotgun shut, Hardy trained it on him. "I can kill you too, tin star. Easy as pie."

Cripdin thrust out his hands as if to ward off a blast. "Don't! I'm begging you!"

"Pitiful," Hardy said. He glanced at Fargo and chuckled. "This is why we ain't been caught and never will be."

"You not be careless," Niyan warned him, covering the posse.

"Don't tell me you're worried about these infants?" Hardy said, and laughed with scorn. "Look at them. They have yellow streaks a mile wide."

"Not take chances," Niyan said.

Hardy sighed and regarded the prone figures with contempt. "You heard the breed. Shuck your hardware. Do it slow unless you want your brains splattered the same as your friend."

Turtles could not have done it slower.

"That leaves you, marshal," Hardy said when they had all complied except Cripdin.

"Go easy on those triggers," the lawman said as he carefully pulled Fargo's Colt from under his belt with two fingers and dropped it in the grass. He did the same with his own revolver.

"There now," Hardy said, and let the muzzles of his shotgun dip. "Let's get down to business. What are all of you doin' here, anyhow?" He paused. "As if I can't guess."

"Jennifer Hemmings," Cripdin said, and caught himself. "Or maybe I should say Jennifer Blasingame."

"How'd you find out who she is?" Hardy asked. "Cord wanted it kept secret."

Cripdin and most of the posse stared at Fargo.

"*You* told them?" Hardy said. "Cord won't like that much."

"I thought he was lying," Cripdin said. "He wanted us to turn around and head back."

"You should have listened," Hardy said.

"What are you fixing to do?"

"I should gun you," Hardy said. "Were it up to me, I would. But Cord says we're not to kill unless we have to. So I reckon you can go on livin' for a spell."

The relief on Cripdin's face and some of the others was almost comical.

"Sort of," Hardy said, and smirked.

"How do you mean?"

"Leave your horses and weapons here and start back on foot."

"Be reasonable," Cripdin said. "It will take a week or better. We'd never make it."

"There are plenty of streams to drink from and game is everywhere," Hardy said.

"How can we kill anything without our guns?"

"You'll think of somethin'," Hardy said.

"It's the same as murder, I tell you," the marshal angrily declared.

Hardy wagged the shotgun. "On your feet."

"You want us to start back *now*?"

"I do," Hardy said, and thumbed back a hammer. "Niyan will follow you a ways to see that you don't try to double back."

Cripdin gazed out over the vast pool of pitch black. "We might run into a bear or those wolves we keep hearing—"

"Or you could trip and stub your damn toe," Hardy said. "On your way before I change my mind."

Panic-stricken, the posse nonetheless rose and shuffled away, giving the outlaws wide berths.

"I don't make it back, a federal marshal will come to investigate," Cripdin said. "They're not as easy to deal with as me."

"That could take months, if ever," Hardy said. "Off you go."

"What if I give you the money in my poke?" Cripdin offered. "There must be twenty dollars or better."

"That much?" Hardy scoffed.

Fargo was biding his time. They had forgotten about him. Even Niyan. In a few steps he could snatch up his Colt and turn the tables.

"Why am I still lookin' at you?" Hardy growled at the posse. "You'd better skedaddle while you can."

"I won't forget this," Cripdin blustered.

"Niyan," Hardy said, "if he opens his damn mouth again, shoot him in it."

"I do," the breed said.

Like men walking to their own execution, the towns-men moved off into the night.

Niyan melted after them.

"It's just you and me now," Hardy said, and sank cross-legged to the ground on the other side of the fire.

Fargo was curious. "Why am I still breathing?"

"Cord would like some words with you. He sent the breed and me to town to get you but we saw this fire and came for a look-see. Lucky us, huh? It's spared us havin' to go all the way to Meridian."

"Why does he want to see me?" Fargo asked. As if he couldn't guess.

"Let's put it this way." Hardy chuckled. "I wouldn't care to be in your boots. Not after what you did to Constance."

"Tassy shot her."

"By mistake, we hear. His other gal, Jennifer, told him all about it."

"Then he shouldn't blame me."

"You'll find out how Cord feels about it soon enough." Hardy picked up a tin cup that had fallen from the hand of a posse member. He wiped the rim on his pants and refilled it.

Fargo was surprised that the outlaw didn't pick up all the weapons lying about. He wondered if Hardy had left them there on purpose; Hardy *wanted* him to try to grab one to use as an excuse to blow him in half and justify the killing to Blasingame.

"I bet right about now you're wishin' you never came to these parts," Hardy said.

"I regret Constance and Tassy dying," Fargo confessed.

"You'll regret it even more before too long," Hardy said, and leaned forward. "You see, I know somethin' about Cord that you don't. That hardly anyone does except us that ride with him and that bitch of a wife of his."

"I'm listening."

"No," Hardy said. "I won't spoil the surprise." He sat back and drank and didn't say anything for several minutes.

Fargo didn't try anything.

After a while Hardy sighed and upended the cup and threw it to the ground. "You're a disappointment, mister. I took you to have more sand."

"I had a hunch," Fargo said.

"I was that obvious? Damn. I was hopin' to save Cord the trouble." Hardy raised his head and his voice. "You can come on in, Niyan."

The breed seemed to appear out of thin air like a specter. "This one smart."

"Too smart for his own good," Hardy said. Standing, he trained the shotgun on Fargo. "Tie his hands in front of him so he can ride and we'll take him with us."

Fargo wasn't hankering to commit suicide; he didn't resist.

"This is a fine mess, and it's all that bitch's doin'," Hardy said. "Why in hell Cord doesn't let us do her in, I'll never know."

"Him still like her," Niyan said while tightening a knot.

"I gave him credit for more sense," Hardy said. "Women ain't worth the bother. Nothin' is ever good enough for them. They nag and they bitch, and when you don't do as they want they treat you like you're a simpleton."

Niyan went into the dark and returned with their horses. They climbed on, and Hardy commanded Fargo to mount the Ovaro.

Fargo grinned at their mistake. He could ride with his hands tied in front of him as well as if his hands were free. He'd make a break the first chance he got.

"Almost forgot," Hardy said. Uncoiling his rope, he kneed his horse over and proceeded to rig a loop and drop it over Fargo's head and neck and make the loop snug. As if he had read Fargo's thoughts, he laughed and said, "Try to get away now."

With Niyan in front of him and Hardy close behind holding the other end of the rope, they started to the north.

"What about the posse's horses?" Fargo asked.

"What about them?" Hardy returned. "We don't need any."

"And the guns?"

"We don't need those, either. Shut the hell up and ride."

More than an hour went by. The stars glittered in a clear sky, and now and then the wind gusted.

Hardy had been quiet the whole time but now he remarked on how much he'd liked blowing the townsman's head off. "There's nothin' like buckshot for gettin' the job done."

"And you don't have to be much of a shot," Fargo said. "All you have to do is point and squeeze."

"Tryin' to get my goat, are you?" Hardy laughed. "It won't work."

Fargo was curious about something and said, "I'm surprised you're willing to take orders from a man like Blasingame."

"That won't work either."

"He doesn't carry a gun. He lets the rest of you do all the killing. Why ride with him?"

"He's got more brains than I ever will. And he stands by us. That there makes him worth his weight in gold."

Niyan grunted in agreement.

"The thing you should be thinkin' about," Hardy said, "is that you have stepped in it up to your neck. The townsfolk hate you. Glenda is usin' you. Jennifer blames you for her sister dyin' and Cord can't wait to show you how he feels about losin' his little girl." He made a tsk-tsk sound. "Fact is, I can't think of anyone I'd rather not be than you."

"Thanks," Fargo said.

"Tell me. Is that bounty money worth all this?"

"It's not worth having to listen to you."

"Talk tough all you want. But if you know any prayers, now's the time to waste your breath sayin' 'em." And Hardy laughed.

20

No two mountain peaks were alike. Some were bare rock, others had timber to their summits. Some were spikes thrust at the heavens, others jagged or rounded. In the Tetons there was a mountain the Indians called "Buffalo Head" because the summit bore an uncanny resemblance to a buff. In Arizona a mountaintop with a silhouette remarkably like the head of a horse was called "Horse Mountain." And here, in the Shadow Mountains, reared a peak shaped like the head of a bird.

Niyan and Hardy made straight for it.

Fargo found out why when they entered the mouth of a canyon that couldn't be seen until they were right on top of it. The canyon wound along the bottom of the bird-peaked mountain and came to end in a three-sided box hemmed by cliffs.

The surface of a spring gleamed in the bright light of the midday sun. Cottonwoods grew in profusion and so did plenty of grass for graze. A cabin had been built, with log walls and a stone chimney. There was a corral for their horses, and of all things, an outhouse.

Nesbit was seated on a stump with a rifle across his legs, keeping watch down the canyon. He stood and gave a nod of greeting to Niyan and Hardy.

Davies was on the top rail of the corral, whittling. On seeing them, he closed his folding knife and hopped down.

Mills was chopping firewood. He set the ax down and came over.

Cord Blasingame stepped from the cabin. As usual, he wasn't armed. "So I was right to have you keep an eye on our back trail," he said as Niyan and Hardy came to a stop. "He was tracking us."

"He wasn't the only one lookin' for us," Hardy said, and related his run-in with the posse.

"You shot one?" Blasingame interrupted when Hardy came to that point. "I've told you before. The fewer of them we kill, the less incentive they have to come after us."

"I don't even know what incentive means," Hardy said. "He was throwin' down on me. What else was I to do?"

"You did right," Blasingame said. He stared up at Fargo and smiled but there was no warmth in it. "We meet again."

"Where's Jennifer?" Fargo asked.

"Inside," Blasingame replied. "And you're a fine one to show concern for her after what you did to Constance."

"Tassy shot her. Not me."

"It was you that threw her aim off. Jen told me all about it." Blasingame motioned at the others. "Get him off his horse and bring him inside, if you would."

Mills and Davies did the honors, Mills with his hand on the hilt of his bowie.

They had gone to some trouble to make the cabin homey. A bearskin rug lay in front of the fireplace. A lamp sat in the center of the table. Their bedrolls were piled in a corner.

Jennifer was tied to a chair over near the far wall. She didn't appear to have been harmed. "They caught you," she said.

"This is how you treat your flesh and blood?" Fargo said to Blasingame.

"She kept trying to leave."

Jennifer glared at her father. "I don't want to be here. You have no right to keep me against my will."

"I have every right when it's for your own good," Blasingame said. "I've lost one daughter. I'm not about to lose another."

"Nothing will happen to me," Jennifer said.

"You don't know that."

Jennifer turned back to Fargo. "Isn't it touching, how devoted he is?"

"Don't start with that again," Blasingame said. "I walked out on your mother, not on you and your sister."

"You left us all the same," Jennifer said, "and I'll never forgive you."

Blasingame instructed Mills and Davies to tie Fargo to a chair, too. "We don't want him slipping away like he did the last time."

Jennifer asked a question very much on Fargo's own mind. "What are you fixing to do with him?"

"He'll be our guest for a short while," Blasingame said. "And then he won't be."

"I don't like the sound of that," Jennifer said.

Neither did Fargo. But with Hardy and Niyan covering him, there was nothing for it but to submit to being tied. When Mills and Davies finished and stepped back, Blasingame came over and stood in front of him.

"I want you to know I don't blame you entirely for Connie's death. Part of the blame is mine."

"I don't recollect you being there," Fargo said.

"I had you in my power once and let you live. If I'd done as some of the others wanted and let them kill you, my daughter would still be alive."

"Don't be so hard on yourself, Cord," Mills said. "How were you to know?"

"I played at being nice to him and it cost me," Blasingame said.

"Played?" Fargo repeated.

A flinty gleam came into Blasingame's eyes as he bent so they were face to face. "Did you honestly think I was as

121

kindly as all that? Did you think that men like these"—and he swept an arm at the killers and cutthroats—"would follow someone who wasn't just like them?"

"I did think it strange," Fargo admitted.

Blasingame's smile became downright vicious. "I learned a long time ago that if you treat people as if they're your best friend, you can get them to do damn near anything."

"It's not all pretend," Mills said.

"Not with you and the others, no. We're pards." Blasingame straightened. "But everyone else, I use it like you use your bowie and Hardy his shotgun. It's a weapon to keep folks in line."

"I told you he was smart," Hardy said to Fargo.

"Let's go have a drink," Blasingame said to them, and they trooped out.

Fargo tested the ropes. He couldn't move his arms or legs the barest fraction. "Damn."

"I'm sorry," Jennifer said.

"For what?" Fargo asked while straining every sinew in his body.

"You came after me, didn't you? You wouldn't be in the fix you're in if not for me."

"I'm in the fix I'm in," Fargo said, "because I tried to do the posse a favor." Never again, he vowed.

"My father has been saying the craziest things," Jennifer said. "How he wants him and me to be like a normal father and daughter. How he wants me to stay with them from here on out. Can you believe it?"

Fargo was willing to believe people would do just about anything, but he held his tongue.

"He blames my mother more than you. He says she shouldn't have come after him. She should have left well enough alone."

Fargo debated rocking his chair until it tipped over in

the hope it would shatter and he could wrest free. Only the outlaws were bound to hear.

"They hate each other, you know, my mother and father," Jennifer had gone on. "When you get right down to it, this whole thing is about hate."

"For me it's about breathing."

"If you were free, what would you do?"

"Kill the sons of bitches."

"My father too?"

"Him most of all," Fargo said. Now that he knew the nice act for what it was, he realized that Cord Blasingame was as deadly as the rest. So what if Blasingame had the others squeeze the trigger for him? It was the same as if Blasingame did it.

"That's what I'm afraid of," Jennifer said. "I want your word you won't."

"Can't give it to you," Fargo said. It wasn't about the bounty anymore. It was personal.

"Please. Give me your solemn promise that you won't hurt my father."

Fargo looked at her.

"If you do, I'll take you with me," Jennifer said. She glanced at the front door. Then, to his surprise, she moved her right arm away from the chair. "I wriggled it free hours ago. They didn't tie me as tight as they tied you."

"Lucky you."

"Don't be mean." Jennifer placed her arm flush with the chair, holding the rope so it appeared she was still tied. "Will you or won't you?"

"I can kill everybody else?"

"You're awful bloodthirsty. Has anyone ever told you that?"

Fargo couldn't believe she was haggling with his life. "They're fixing to kill *me*."

"All right. I don't care about the others. They've treated

123

me decent but only because my father makes them. You can kill whoever else you want. Satisfied?"

"Get me the hell out of this," Fargo said, and shook the chair.

"Hold your horses. It will be a while yet. You heard my father."

Fargo wasn't so sure. And he disliked being helpless. He disliked it more than just about anything.

"I figured to wait until they turn in."

"That won't be for hours," Fargo said. Far too long.

"I'll stall him. I'll beg him not to do anything to you."

"You're playing with my life."

Jennifer mulled that while staring at the door. From outside came voices and gruff laughter.

"Do it now," Fargo urged her.

"Don't rush me, consarn you."

Without warning the door opened and in strode Cord Blasingame. He was holding a whiskey bottle and took a swig and grinned. "Having fun?"

"I don't like being trussed like this," Jennifer said. "If you really cared about me, you'd set me free."

"Forget it, girl. We both know you'd bolt the first chance you got." Blasingame leaned against the table and regarded Fargo like a cat about to play with a mouse. "Any regrets?"

"Go to hell."

"Now, now. Pettiness won't do you any favors. Do you want it quick or slow?"

"Untie me and give me a gun."

"Do I look insane?" Blasingame laughed. "The last person I did in was a bank guard. He tried to back-shoot me when we robbed the bank so we brought him with us. He begged for me to give him a gun, too. I burned him alive."

"Father, you didn't," Jennifer gasped.

"It was quite the spectacle."

Fargo tried to recollect if he ever heard an outlaw use the word "spectacle" before.

Blasingame set down the bottle and straightened. "I suppose we should get to it."

Just then, from down the canyon, came a shout. "You there! This is Marshal Theodore Cripdin! We have you trapped! Surrender or else!"

21

"What the hell?" Cord Blasingame blurted, and was out the door in a heartbeat.

There was a shot, and a cry, and then a flurry of rifle and pistol fire that ended when Blasingame hollered, "Stop firing! Stop firing!"

"Where did the marshal come from?" Jennifer asked. "How did he find this place?"

"Get me loose," Fargo said. "Now." He needed to take advantage of the distraction while it lasted.

"You haven't promised yet," Jennifer said.

"To hell with you then," Fargo said. Bracing both feet, he stood, the chair forcing him to stoop slightly.

Coiling, he jumped straight up. In midair he tilted his body back so that his full weight came down on top of the chair as it crashed to the floor. He heard a loud crack, and splintering. The rear legs had broken but not the front; his own legs were still tied fast.

Grunting from the effort, Fargo rolled onto his side and from there managed to heave to his feet again.

"Promise me," Jennifer said. She had freed one hand and was prying at the knots to the rope that bound her other arm to the chair.

Outside, Marshal Cripdin and Cord Blasingame were shouting at one another. Something about the lawman giving the outlaws ten minutes to throw down their guns and come out with their hands in the air.

"I don't want my father hurt," Jennifer said. "I don't care what he's done. He's still my father."

Fargo tensed and jumped. This time when he crashed down, the already weakened chair cracked and broke in several places. A wrench, and his left arm was loose but still tied to the part of the chair that had broken off. Quickly, he began working on the rope around his other wrist.

"Didn't you hear me? Why won't you say anything?"

"I'm like your father," Fargo said.

"I don't understand."

"I'm tired of being nice." Fargo pried with fierce fervor; any moment, one of the outlaws might come in.

Down the canyon, Marshal Cripdin shouted, "We have you boxed in, Blasingame. Try to escape and we'll blast you from your saddles."

Someone laughed. It sounded like Hardy.

"I'm told there are only six of you, marshal," Blasingame yelled back.

"So?" Cripdin hollered.

"Your posse is made up of shopkeepers and a stableman, I understand. Do you honestly think you're a match for us?"

"We have rifles and we're not bad shots," Cripdin said.

"A lawman shouldn't lie," Blasingame said. "None of you could hit the broad side of a barn if your lives depended on it."

"Try us," Cripdin said.

Fargo, meanwhile, had freed his right hand and was working on his feet.

"There," Jennifer said, and stood. She moved to the door and peeked out, then came back. "This is your last chance. Give me your word you won't hurt him."

Fargo tugged at a knot. If he could get to the toothpick it would make short shrift of the last ropes.

"Ignoring me, are you? Very well. I'll let my father know you're almost loose."

Fargo looked up. "You wouldn't."

"Ah," Jennifer said, grinning. "That got your attention."

"He'll kill me that much sooner," Fargo said.

"You don't know that. He's too busy with the marshal. He'll probably just tie you again."

"And you," Fargo said, tugging furiously.

"All you had to do was give me your word." Shaking her head, Jennifer turned toward the door.

Lunging, Fargo grabbed her ankles. Before she could think to act or call for help, he jerked her legs out from under her.

Jennifer came down hard on her elbows. She cried out and kicked with both legs, trying to break free, but he held on and pulled her toward him.

"Stop! Let go of me!"

Pinning her legs with his chest, Fargo got an arm around her waist. Jennifer twisted and clawed at his face, raking a cheek.

"Let go, I said!"

Fargo had to silence her. Balling his fist, he struck her flush on the jaw. He held back but he still hit her hard enough that it caused her eyelids to flutter. He would have let go but even though she was dazed and weakened, she tried to crawl toward the door, yelling, "Father! Help me!"

Fargo slugged her again. This time she went limp. He didn't waste a second. As soon as his right leg was free he resorted to the toothpick. Then, standing, he carried Jennifer over near the stove where she would be out of harm's way and gently set her down.

A search for a weapon turned up a butcher knife. That was all. His Henry was still on the Ovaro, so far as he knew, and he didn't know where his Colt had gotten to.

Just then Blasingame yelled, "Use your damn head, Cripdin. We have plenty to eat and the spring to slake our thirst. We can wait you out. Eventually you'll run out of supplies and have to go back to town."

"Why bother waitin'?" Hardy said so that only the outlaws heard. "Why not go finish this?"

"If it comes to that," Blasingame said, "we'll wait until dark and let Niyan deal with them."

"Them easy to kill," the breed said.

The lawman gave a holler of his own. "I can send one of my men for help. We'll have twenty more rifles in no time."

"Who are you kidding?" Blasingame responded. "It'll take days for your man to reach Meridian. Do you expect us to twiddle our thumbs until he gets back?"

Standing to one side of the door with the butcher knife in one hand and the Arkansas toothpick in the other, Fargo peered out. He saw several of the outlaws right away; Cord Blasingame and Mills were over at the horses, behind a sorrel, using it for cover; Hardy was behind a stump; Nesbit had hunkered behind a boulder.

There was no sign of Niyan or Davies.

A head poked out past the first bend down the canyon. "I gave you your chance," Marshal Cripdin hollered. "What happens next is on your shoulders." He quickly pulled back.

Fargo needed to reach the Ovaro. He crouched and started to ease out of the cabin when he spotted a figure snaking along the bottom of the canyon wall. It was Niyan, halfway to the bend. Once Niyan reached it, he could pick off the posse with his Spencer.

Fargo almost shouted a warning but it would only get him shot. Instead, he crept toward the nearest outlaw, Nesbit.

Nesbit took off his hat and raised his head for a look-see.

Fargo moved faster. He figured to bury the butcher knife in the outlaw's back, reclaim his Henry, and cut loose on the others. He glanced at Blasingame and Mills and Hardy to be sure they hadn't looked back and seen him. He thought to glance at Niyan, too, and stopped cold in his tracks.

The breed had stopped crawling. Niyan must have glanced

back and seen him and was raising the Spencer to his shoulder.

Fargo threw himself down just as the rifle boomed.

Blasingame, Hardy and the other outlaws all looked toward Niyan, wondering why he had fired.

In a burst of speed, Fargo raced for the cabin. He was almost there when the Spencer cracked again. So did a revolver from over at the horses. As he went through the doorway, lead smacked a log inches from his elbow. Ducking inside, he slammed the door. There was no bar, no bolt. He put his back to it but thought better of the idea and darted to one side.

No sooner did he move than several shots crashed through the door.

Fargo went to the window. It had no glass and just an old piece of blanket for a curtain. Carefully moving it, he risked a peek.

The outlaws were all facing the cabin. Niyan had turned and was crawling back.

"We should rush him," Hardy hollered to Blasingame. "He doesn't have a gun."

"Stay put," the outlaw leader said. "We show ourselves, the posse will open up."

"They can't shoot worth a damn. You said so yourself."

"Stay put anyway." Blasingame cupped a hand to his mouth. "Jennifer? Can you hear me in there?"

Fargo glanced over. She was still unconscious.

"Jennifer? Answer me?" Blasingame took a step toward the cabin but Mills grabbed his arm and said something.

"Fargo!" Blasingame shouted. "Why doesn't she answer? What have you done to her?"

"I've gagged her," Fargo lied.

"Let her talk to me so I know she's all right."

"I'll make a deal," Fargo proposed. "Your daughter for my horse and my guns."

"Don't listen to him," Hardy butted in. "He harms a hair on her head, he's as good as dead and he knows it."

"My horse and my guns," Fargo said, "and I'll ride out and never come back."

"I don't believe you," Blasingame said. "And I want to talk to her, damn you."

Jennifer groaned.

"If I let you talk, I get my horse and my guns?"

"Yes," Blasingame said.

"No!" Hardy shouted. "He tries to ride off, I'll blow him to hell and back."

They began to argue.

Fargo went over to Jennifer. Her jaw was swollen and bruised. He set the butcher knife behind him and touched her arm and her eyes slowly opened. She tried to speak and groaned louder.

"I hurt something awful."

Sliding a hand under her, Fargo boosted her up and over to the chair she had been tied to. "Take it easy while your head clears."

"You hit me."

"I'll do it again if you force me."

Gingerly rubbing her chin, Jennifer said glumly, "And to think, I let you have your way with me. I won't make that mistake twice."

Blasingame picked that moment to shout, "Jennifer? Can you hear me? Come out here."

She began to stand.

"No," Fargo said, putting a hand on her shoulder. "You're not going anywhere."

"That's what you think," Jennifer said, and drove her foot between his legs.

22

Pain exploded clear down to Fargo's toes. Clutching himself, he staggered. He grabbed at Jennifer with his other hand but she sidestepped and was past and to the door before he recovered enough to take a step of his own. "Don't," he said.

"Go to hell." Jennifer flung herself outside and there were shouts.

When Fargo reached the window she was over at the horses with Blasingame and Mills.

Blasingame had his hand to her chin and was turning her face from side to side. Glaring toward the cabin, he hollered, "You hurt her, you son of a bitch."

Fargo didn't respond. What good would it do?

"Hear me!" Blasingame cried, but not to Fargo, to the other outlaws. "I'll give a thousand dollars of my own money to any of you who kill him."

Fargo swore. He supposed there was a certain irony in having a bounty put on his head by a man who had a bounty on his own but he was in no mood to appreciate it. He saw Nesbit suddenly rise and charge toward the cabin, and moved to the doorway. He'd left the butcher knife on the floor but he still had his toothpick and he held it low against his leg, ready to thrust.

Nesbit didn't slow, didn't hesitate. He burst inside looking right and left, his rifle in front of him.

Fargo stabbed him in the chest and simultaneously thrust his foot out, tripping him. He felt the blade strike bone and knew it had been deflected by a rib. Then Nesbit was on the floor and rolling, the rifle's muzzle rising. Fargo threw himself aside. The rifle boomed and the slug struck the wall. He sprang, stabbing at Nesbit's heart, only to have the rifle stock catch him across his ribs and smash him to the floor.

"You cut me!" Nesbit roared, and came at him in a frenzy, swinging the rifle like a club.

Fargo ducked, rolled, made it to his knees. A blow to his shoulder knocked him down again. The next moment Nesbit was straddling him and pressing the barrel across his throat. He pushed at the rifle but couldn't force it up. He couldn't breathe and his lungs protested with new pain.

"That thousand is mine," Nesbit gloated, spittle flecking his lips.

Fargo speared the toothpick into the outlaw's throat, and twisted. Wet drops spattered his face and his shirt.

Nesbit, recoiling, tried to say something but all that came out of his mouth was blood. He let go of the rifle and grabbed at his neck in a bid to staunch the flow. Lurching to his feet, he tottered toward the door.

Fargo grabbed at his leg, and missed.

Nesbit stumbled outside.

Fargo made it to his feet. He left the rifle on the floor; it was a single-shot and he didn't have ammunition for it. He moved to the window.

Nesbit was staggering toward the horses. Hardy cursed in rage, and Niyan was returning on the run. Out at the bend, Marshal Cripdin was watching but not saying or doing anything.

Fargo did some swearing of his own. If the lawman had any sense he'd rush the outlaws while they were focused on Nesbit and the cabin.

Nesbit reached an arm toward Cord Blasingame, tried to speak, and pitched to the ground. He broke into convulsions that lasted longer than any Fargo ever saw. He was still convulsing when Niyan shot him in the head to put him out of his misery.

Fargo leaned his back to the wall and put his hands on his legs. He'd killed another of them but there were five left and they had guns and he didn't. It hit him they might rush him and he looked out again just as Marshal Cripdin gave a yell.

"Only five of you now, Blasingame. You still have a chance to surrender."

"Go to hell," the outlaw leader replied.

"You think you can wait us out but you can't."

"Shut up, you damn useless bastard."

"I'm about to show you how mistaken you are," Cripdin shouted. "I won't be the laughingstock of Meridian much longer."

"You're going to take a long time to die," Blasingame vowed.

Fargo was grateful for the exchange. It bought him time. Neither Mills nor Hardy made a move toward the cabin. Nor did Niyan, who had taken cover behind a log. Sooner or later, though, they were bound to try.

Fargo had an inspiration. The rifle was empty but they didn't know that. Retrieving it, he came back to the window, shoved the barrel out where they could see it, and hollered, "I'll shoot the first son of a bitch who tries to come in here."

That should dissuade them a while, he figured. But he was still trapped and needed to think of something, fast.

He searched the cabin again, more thoroughly. There was no ammunition anywhere. He turned to the window to keep an eye on them and his gaze fell on a lantern. It gave him an idea.

He went to the broken chair, gathered up the pieces, and careful not to show himself, threw them out the door a few feet in front of the cabin. He did the same with the other chair.

"What in hell are you doing?" Cord Blasingame shouted.

Fargo took a couple of blankets and added them to the pile. In his search he'd found some lucifers. He stroked one and lit the lantern.

He'd like to wait until dark but he didn't dare. Too much could happen.

Blasingame must have guessed what he was up to. "Cover the doorway, boys. When he makes his break, shoot the bastard down."

Fargo hurled the lantern at the pile. It shattered, and flames spread across the blankets, growing rapidly. Smoke rose, a lot of it, so much that in no time a cloud formed, and because there was no wind it hugged the ground—and the front of the cabin.

Flattening, Fargo crawled out the door and bore to the right along the wall. He made it to the corner without being seen and without shots ringing out, and once he was around to the side, he rose into a crouch. So far, so good.

"Do you see him?" Blasingame yelled.

"No," Hardy replied. "I can't see a damn thing. It's as thick as soup."

The smoke spread. As it overlapped the cabin, Fargo moved toward some cottonwoods. He stayed alert for sign of Niyan. The breed was the best of them, and could be anywhere.

Luck favored him. He reached the cottonwoods, and cover. His throat was dry and he could use some water, and he was hungry as hell, but they were the least of his worries.

The smoke had spread outward past the boulder, hiding Hardy, and was creeping toward the horses. The fire was about out, though.

Fargo crouched, debating what to do. Movement high on the canyon wall caught his eye. He looked, and couldn't believe what he was seeing: a pair of posse members with rifles.

Cripdin was proving to be more competent than Fargo imagined. The lawman must have sent them up there not long after he arrived.

But Blasingame must have had the same idea.

More movement drew Fargo's gaze to a figure slinking toward them. It was Davies.

The posse men were peering down at Blasingame and the other outlaws.

Fargo wanted to shout to warn them but it would give him away. He stepped from behind the cottonwood and waved his arms to try to get their attention but they didn't see him.

Davies was almost on them.

One of the posse members took aim in the direction of the horses, and Blasingame.

Quick as thought, Davies shot him in the back, shifted, and shot the other one.

Fargo dropped from sight. So much for the posse having the advantage.

Blasingame waved to Davies and Davies waved back. Turning toward the bend, Blasingame laughed and shouted, "Any other bright ideas, marshal?"

"They were family men, damn you," Cripdin yelled.

"Then they shouldn't have joined your posse," Blasingame said.

"You'll hang for this."

"Come to your senses, you idiot," Blasingame said. "You only have a few men left. So I'll tell you what. Mount up and leave, right this minute, and I won't hold this against you."

"No."

"Maybe you should ask the men you deputized how they feel," Blasingame said. "Do they want to live or do they want to die?"

"You are a miserable son of a bitch."

Blasingame laughed. "Hardy has his shotgun and Mills his bowie but I have my words. They're my weapon." He raised his voice. "Do you hear me back there, you men? Think of your loved ones. Your wives and your children. Don't you want to see them again? To hold them in you arms?"

"Shut the hell up," Cripdin hollered.

"You've done your best," Blasingame went on. "But now you're outnumbered and when dark falls I'll send the breed in and you know what will happen. Leave, now, while you still can. Go home to your families. I give you my word we won't come after you."

Muffled shouts from past the bend ended with the drum of hooves. Marshal Cripdin swore luridly.

Blasingame chortled. "How many do you have left, tin star? I bet it's just you."

Cripdin didn't answer.

"Better go with them," Blasingame said. "Or I'll have the breed stake you out and carve on you."

"You don't scare me," Cripdin hollered.

"Could be I don't." Blasingame laughed some more; he was enjoying himself. "But I bet the breed does. I bet he scares the piss out of you. So smarten up and go, you damned jackass."

Fargo waited. It wasn't a minute more that hooves pounded, fading rapidly.

"Do you hear that, Fargo, wherever you are?" Blasingame shouted. "It's just you now, and us. You know what that means?"

Fargo glided through the cottonwoods and into the shadow of the canyon wall. Knives against guns was next to hopeless but he'd be damned if he'd give up without a struggle.

"Nothing to say?" Blasingame taunted. "Don't want to give yourself away? That's all right. Ready or not, here we come."

23

Move, Fargo's mind warned, and he did, along the wall, staying always in shadow. He was across the canyon from the horses, and the Ovaro. He needed to reach them but with Davies up on the rim and the others hunting him, he'd be hard pressed to do it unseen.

Inspiration struck, and he moved toward the far bend instead.

The smoke was thinning.

Someone coughed, and Hardy appeared at the front of the cabin. He'd just come from inside and yelled, "He's not in the cabin, Cord!"

"Didn't reckon he would be," Blasingame replied. "Watch yourselves. I don't need to remind you how dangerous he is."

"So am I," Hardy said as he moved toward the cottonwoods Fargo had vacated.

Fargo went faster. Except for a dull ache between his legs he felt fine. He told himself there were only five of them. He told himself it wasn't as hopeless as it seemed.

Cord Blasingame liked to hear himself talk. "Fargo, I know you can hear me. For killing Connie and hurting Jen, I'll see you dead if it takes the rest of my days."

Fargo imagined putting a slug through Blasingame's brainpan to shut him up, and grinned.

"Any sign of him, Davies?" Blasingame hollered.

Davies rose up and shook his head.

Fargo had to remember to keep an eye on the rim. He came to a belt of brush and weeds and sank to his belly.

Blasingame and Jennifer were hurrying toward the cabin. Mills followed, leading some of the horses. One was the Ovaro.

Hardy was in the cottonwoods.

A sense of unease came over Fargo. He'd lost track of Niyan. It could be the breed had spotted him and was stalking him. He hoped to hell not.

The bend. Fargo concentrated on the bend. Pumping his elbows and his knees, he reached it and slid around and almost immediately a Spencer was shoved in his face.

"You!" Marshal Theodore Cripdin blurted.

"I thought I heard you ride off," Fargo said.

"That was the last of my posse," Cripdin said. He lowered his rifle. "Sorry. You gave me a scare, coming out of nowhere."

Rising, Fargo brushed dirt from his shirt and nodded at the lawman's holster. "Any chance you'd let me have that?"

"Why not? I still have my rifle." Cripdin palmed the Smith & Wesson and handed it over. "You probably won't believe this but I'm awful glad to see you."

"How did you find this place?"

"That night Hardy shot Floyd and made us go off on foot, we only went a short way. As soon as Niyan turned back, we stopped and waited for daylight. We were all mad about Floyd and decided we weren't going back to town empty-handed."

"You did good," Fargo said.

"It wasn't easy. The tracks were fresh but none of us were trackers. We stuck at it, though, and damned if we didn't find this canyon, and the rest you know." Cripdin scowled. "Everything was going fine until the rest of them lit a shuck. Damn that Blasingame, anyhow."

"What did you hope to do alone?"

Cripdin shrugged. "I don't have a plan. I only know I'm

sick and tired of everyone looking down their noses at me. I figure that if I can take Cord Blasingame back, I'll get some respect."

"That's a tall order." Fargo checked on the outlaws. Not a single one was in sight. Not even Davies. "Where the hell?"

"What is it?"

Fargo told him.

"It's the breed who worries me most," Cripdin said. "Folks say he's a ghost. That he can sneak up on you and slit your throat before you know he's there."

"He worries me, too," Fargo admitted. He hefted the Smith & Wesson. It was a good revolver but he'd rather have his Colt.

"How's the girl? I saw her come running out of the cabin."

"It looks as if she's taken her father's side in this. She doesn't want him hurt."

"I still can't get over it. Her mother sure pulled the wool over everyone's eyes."

Fargo was watching for Niyan and instead saw Hardy come out of the cottonwoods and cross to the cabin.

"Are you hungry? I have jerky in my saddlebags. And water in my canteen."

Fargo was grateful for both. He drank a few mouthfuls and had two pieces of jerky. As he chewed he said, "I might have been too hard on you back in town." Which was as close as he'd come to an apology.

"It's not as if you're the only one who has ever treated me that way."

"I thought you and Blasingame might be in cahoots," Fargo mentioned.

"Hell no. A lot of townsfolk turn the other cheek because they think he's such a nice cuss, for an outlaw. I always thought different. Robbing is robbing and killing is killing. I don't care how nice he is."

"They have a man up top—"

"I know."

"—who could be working his way around to get a shot at us."

Cripdin glanced up so sharply, it was a wonder his neck didn't snap. "I hadn't thought of that. What do you suggest?"

Fargo had been thinking. "They're not as smart as they think they are. This is a box canyon. I say we wait at the mouth for them to come out and pick them off as they do."

"Blasingame isn't stupid. He'll wait until after the sun goes down and slip out without us knowing. Or sic that damn breed on us."

"Do you have a better idea?"

"Can't say as I do, no."

"Then let's give it a try."

They walked, with Cripdin leading his horse.

Fargo kept watch on the rim but Davies didn't show himself.

The lawman was quiet a while, then cleared his throat. "My posse sure proved useless."

"They tried their best."

"Best, hell. Blasingame put the fear of dying into them and they tucked tail and ran."

"Clerks against killers," Fargo said. "They wouldn't have stood a prayer."

"Why are you defending them? I deputized them. They should have stuck by me, come what may."

"A lot of men talk bigger than they are."

"There you go again," Cripdin said. "All I know is they left me to deal with the outlaws alone." He paused. "What about the girl? When they make their break, what do we do about her?"

"Nothing."

"But what if she gets in the way?" Cripdin persisted. "It'll be Constance all over again."

Fargo winced. "Let's hope not."

"I still can't get over her siding with Blasingame. Kin or no kin."

"We should keep quiet," Fargo said.

For once Cripdin took the hint.

There was still no sign of Davies up high. Fargo was more concerned about Niyan; the breed could be anywhere. The next bend they came to, he went around it and stopped. Putting a finger to his lips, he squatted to wait.

Cripdin hunkered and whispered, "What are we doing?"

"I'm not fond of lead in the back."

They watched a while, until Fargo was sure they weren't being stalked.

"I wouldn't have thought of doing that," Cripdin said as they moved on. "I'm not much at this fighting business, I'm afraid."

"I've had a little practice at it," Fargo told him.

"You're a regular hellion. Since you showed up, people have been dying right and left."

"They were dying before I came."

Cripdin plodded another minute before remarking, "Blasingame must want you dead awful bad on account of his other girl."

"You can shut up now."

The mouth of the canyon wasn't ideal for Fargo's purpose. It was too wide, for one thing, and not open enough, for another. He took Cripdin into the trees beyond and together they gathered firewood. As he was kindling tinder into flame, the lawman did what he liked to do best—complain.

"I don't see why we're making a fire. They'll spot it right off and know where we are."

"We want them to."

Cripdin shook his head. "Why is it I can't hardly savvy half the things you do?"

Fargo puffed on a finger of flame and added fuel. When

the fire was crackling to his satisfaction, he led Cripdin into the trees to find downed limbs and dragged a few back.

"Stranger and stranger," Cripdin said.

"Fetch your bedroll," Fargo directed.

It took some doing to make the blanket-covered branches look real enough to fool anyone. Close up it was obvious but by then the outlaws would be in their gun sights.

"I get it now," Cripdin said as they arranged the second fake. "But I doubt Blasingame will fall for it. You expect him to believe we went to sleep with him and his men after us?"

"They'll be curious enough to come close," Fargo expressed his hope.

"And then we gun them?"

"We sure as hell do."

After that there was nothing to do but pick their spots and wait for the sun to sink.

Fargo debated whether to separate and decided not to. He needed to keep the lawman quiet and still. So they hid under a spruce, lying where they could watch the canyon mouth and spot anyone who came out of it, and see the clearing, too.

"This is the hard part. The waiting," Cripdin said.

Fargo didn't respond.

"What happens if this plan of yours doesn't work?"

"They kill us."

"Damn it. I'm serious. I'd be grateful for an honest answer."

"That was," Fargo said.

24

The sun was an hour above the western horizon when movement stirred Fargo into raising his chin from his forearm. He expected it to be Niyan, who was by far the stealthiest of the outlaws. But it was Hardy, Mills and Davies who appeared, darting from boulder to boulder.

Fargo reached over and poked Cripdin, who had dozed off.

"Eh?" The marshal jerked his head up and looked around in confusion.

"Do or die time," Fargo said.

Cripdin blinked. "Just three of them? Where's Blasingame and the breed and the girl?"

"Those three are enough for now."

Cripdin raised his rifle to his shoulder.

"Not yet," Fargo said. "We want them good and close."

"Not too close, I hope."

The three killers reached the last of the boulders and went to ground. It was ten minutes or more before Hardy crawled partway from behind his and scanned the woods.

"He's seen the fire," Cripdin whispered excitedly.

Hardy turned and beckoned, and Mills and Davies dashed from their boulders to his.

"They'll rush the blankets, I bet," the marshal said.

"Not if they're smart."

They were. Mills broke right, Davies broke left, and Hardy came up the middle, all three low to the ground and weaving as they ran.

"I can hit one," Cripdin said.

"Not yet."

At the trees the outlaws went to ground again.

"Damn it," Cripdin said. "We missed our chance."

"You have a choice," Fargo said. "Hush or eat teeth."

Cripdin hushed.

The breeze had died and the forest was still. A robin warbled and a jay squawked and the fire went on crackling and dancing.

Fargo had to hand it to the outlaws; they snuck in close before they showed themselves.

Davies appeared first. Or, rather, his head did, at the end of a log. He was intent on the blankets.

Hardy materialized behind a pine. His expression said he didn't like the setup.

Fargo didn't see Mills and that bothered him.

Davies looked at Hardy and Hardy gestured for him to stay where he was. Then, the shotgun cocked, Hardy glided to the edge of the clearing.

Fargo extended the Smith & Wesson. A couple more steps, and he couldn't miss.

Hardy was wary. He scoured the woods and stayed where he was.

Fargo heard a click and glanced over. Cripdin had thumbed back the rifle's hammer and was taking aim. "No," he whispered, too late.

The rifle cracked. Hardy dropped and spun and one of the barrels thundered. Limbs above them were slivered by buckshot.

Fargo went to shoot but Hardy was scuttling backward like a crab, and now Davies rose up from behind the log and his rifle blasted.

"I'm hit!" Cripdin cried.

Scrambling around the spruce, Fargo grabbed the back of the lawman's shirt and hauled him ten yards to a thicket. "You damned jackass. You gave us away."

Cripdin had a hand to his left shoulder and tears in his eyes. "God, I hurt. I need a doctor."

"Let me see."

The lawman moved his hand. The slug had torn the sleeve, leaving the tiniest of nicks and a single drop of blood.

"You should be wearing a diaper," Fargo said.

Cripdin craned his neck. "Is that all it is? It feels worse."

"Come on." Fargo jerked him to his feet and shoved. "Run."

They'd taken only a couple of steps when a rifle cracked and a limb next to Fargo shattered. Ducking, he weaved. Cripdin imitated him.

Fargo ran until they came to a shallow gully. Jumping into it, he turned. "We'll make our stand here."

Cripdin was still holding his shoulder. "I'm in no shape for a fight. We should light a shuck."

"On foot? They'd catch us."

"I can run really fast."

Fargo believed him. Cowards made great runners. "Go on if you want but I'm staying."

"Your trick didn't work. This won't either."

Fargo didn't point out that Cripdin was the reason it hadn't. He listened but didn't hear the outlaws. They could be anywhere.

Cripdin fidgeted and gnawed on his lip. He was a rabbit fit to bolt if a fox appeared.

Fargo looked up and down the gully and behind them, and as he swiveled his head to the front, Hardy stepped into the open, leveled the shotgun, and fired both barrels. Flattening, he hollered, "Get down!"

Cripdin had the reflexes of a slug. Buckshot caught him in the same shoulder as the nick and smashed him against the opposite side of the gully. He cried out, and slumped.

Fargo snapped off a shot but Hardy had already taken cover.

"Oh God, oh, God, oh God," Cripdin blubbered. Blood trickled from between his fingers and down his shirt. "They've killed me."

Fargo half wished they had. He tore his gaze from the woods and checked the wound. It was deep but not life-threatening unless infection set in. They needed to clean and bandage it but that would have to wait. "Stay low," Fargo cautioned, and turned.

"Hold on." Cripdin clutched at his arm. "You're not leaving me?"

"To hunt them," Fargo said. He went to slip out of the gully but the lawman held fast.

"Like hell. I'm hurt. You have to stay to protect me."

"Let go."

"You can't leave me here alone. I'll be a sitting duck."

"That's the idea."

"What?"

"You're bait," Fargo said, and clubbed him. He swept the revolver up and around and slammed it against Cripdin's temple. The lawman folded without a sound. Quickly, Fargo grabbed the rifle, flattened, and snaked out of the gully into high grass and through it to an oak. Tucking the Smith & Wesson under his belt, he held the rifle ready.

What he wouldn't give to have his Colt and Henry. He was used to them, and in a fight to the death, any edge was crucial.

Fargo put it from his mind. He'd do the best he could with what he had; that was all a man could ever do.

Vegetation rustled and Hardy reappeared about thirty feet away, eyeing the gully. He stared at it a considerable while and must have decided to throw caution to the wind because he suddenly charged. He had the shotgun cocked and when he came to the top he stopped and pointed the shotgun at Cripdin. "What the hell?" he blurted on seeing that the lawman was unconscious.

Fargo fired. He sent a slug into Hardy's chest, jacked the

lever to feed a cartridge, sent a second slug just below Hardy's sternum.

Hardy staggered. He waved the shotgun in a circle as if unsure where to shoot and finally squeezed both triggers. But the shotgun wasn't pointing anywhere near Fargo. It obliterated a small pine.

Fargo fired a third time.

Trying to break the shotgun open, Hardy crumbled and died.

A rifle shot rang out. Fargo dived, heard the lead strike the oak. He rolled, heaved up and ran. A glance showed Davies taking aim at his back. He threw himself aside as the rifle went off. Landing on his shoulder, he flipped around and fired as Davies took aim again, fired as Davies lurched a step, fired as Davies sought to raise the rifle, fired as Davies pitched onto his face.

In the abrupt silence, Fargo's ears rang. He jacked the lever but the rifle was empty. Casting it away, he drew the Smith & Wesson.

Davies raised his head and opened his mouth but no sounds came out. He died as mute as he had lived.

Rising, Fargo ran to a fir and dropped prone. His blood was racing. Now there was only Mills.

A groan came from the gully. Then an oath. Cripdin was coming around.

Fargo hoped the lawman was smart enough to stay put.

He should have known better.

Mumbling and shaking his head, Cripdin came crawling out on his hands and knees. He sat up and gazed blankly around, as if he didn't know where he was or what he was doing. He put a hand to his temple and tried to rise but couldn't.

The damn fool, Fargo thought. He had to do something. He was half up when he heard the scrape of soles behind him, and spun. Mills was almost on him, the bowie held low. A boot slammed his wrist and the Smith & Wesson went flying.

Mills slashed and Fargo dodged. Mills stabbed, and Fargo sidestepped. The blade thunked into the fir.

Fargo gripped the outlaw's wrist and Mills rammed a fist at his face. He managed to avoid most of the blow but not all; his cheek was jarred.

"You killed my pards!" Mills raged.

The bowie was an inch from Fargo's chest. He strained but Mills was stronger than he looked. Inch by inch the tip came closer.

Fargo sensed that the outlaw was girding to drive the blade into his body. He shifted, and the edge sliced his buckskin shirt. He slammed his knee into Mills's gut but it had no effect. Slamming it into Mills's elbow did. Mills bellowed in pain and fury and his grip weakened, allowing Fargo to wrench on Mills's wrist. Mills cried out and the bowie dropped.

In a flash Fargo caught it by the hilt. Reversing his grip, he plunged the blade up and in.

Mills looked down at himself. "I'll be damned," he blurted. He swayed, said, "I reckon you've done for me."

And collapsed.

Cripdin was trying to stand.

Fargo went over to give him a hand but the lawman pushed him away.

"I don't need your help. Not after what you did." Cripdin saw Hardy's body. "How many?"

"All three."

"That leaves Cord Blasingame and the half-breed." Cripdin gazed toward the canyon. "Where do you suppose they got to?"

Fargo was wondering the same thing.

25

The box canyon lay quiet under the golden light of the newly risen sun. The horses—except for three that were missing—were grazing.

Fargo went to the Ovaro and patted it and freed it from the picket pin the outlaws had used to tether it with the rest.

Fargo found his Colt lying on the ground between the horse string and the cabin. He wiped off the dew, checked that the cylinder had five pills in the wheel, and twirled it into his holster.

Nesbit lay where he had fallen, stiff as a board.

The cabin door was open.

Fargo's Henry lay on the table. Why the outlaws left it puzzled him. But then, Niyan had his Spencer and Blasingame rarely used a gun.

Marshal Cripdin asked the same question he'd asked the night before. "Where do you reckon the other two got to?"

Tracks gave Fargo the answer; three sets of fresh hoofprints.

At the crack of day, the outlaws had led their mounts to a corner of the canyon hidden by cottonwoods. A narrow ledge crisscrossed the seemingly sheer face above. Barely wide enough for a horse, it went clear to the top.

"I hope you're not fixing to climb that," Cripdin said fearfully.

Fargo wasn't.

"Why didn't Blasingame and the others use it when my posse had them boxed in?"

"It's a slow climb," Fargo gauged. "It will probably take half an hour leading a skittish horse." He suspected another reason had even more to do with it. "And they'd be out in the open, easy targets."

"If Blasingame left at first light they can't be that far off," Cripdin realized. "We hurry, we can catch them."

For once Fargo agreed. They set the other horses free, filled their canteens, and helped themselves to some bread and jerky the outlaws left.

A hard gallop brought them out of the canyon and up and around to the rim.

Fargo found the tracks easily enough; they pointed to the south.

"They're heading for Meridian, by God," Cripdin guessed.

Once again Fargo thought he was right.

They pushed their mounts but the outlaws were pushing, too, and by noon they hadn't gained.

Fargo stopped to rest their animals, briefly, and they were on their way again.

By nightfall they still hadn't gained. They made camp on a low ridge. Fargo got a small fire going and put coffee on. He could do without a hot meal but not his coffee.

They searched the sea of darkness for another fire but saw only black.

"They must have made a cold camp," Cripdin said.

"That makes three," Fargo said. "Maybe folks are right. Miracles do happen."

"What in hell are you talking about?"

Fargo returned to their fire and his coffee. "The thing to ask ourselves," he said between swallows, "is why Meridian?"

"Maybe he's taking his daughter back," Cripdin speculated. "Or he wants to see his wife."

151

"See, or worse?"

The lawman stared at him and his eyes widened. "Blasingame must blame her for all that's happened. You're the one who's shot his gang to ribbons but she's the one who sent for you."

"I was told he still cares for her," Fargo mentioned.

"The breed doesn't."

Fargo hadn't considered that. It could be Blasingame would have Niyan do what he couldn't. "I'm turning in as soon as I'm done with this cup," he announced. "Get plenty of sleep. We're fanning the breeze at first light."

He was true to his word.

They didn't push as hard as the day before. It was pointless to ride their mounts into the ground when it would take several days to reach town.

Cripdin, thankfully, didn't talk him to death. The marshal appeared to have a lot on his mind. It wasn't until the night before they would reach Meridian that he revealed what it was.

They were about ready to turn in when the lawman cleared his throat. "I've been thinking. Maybe you're right."

"About?" Fargo said.

"Me. I'm not cut out for this job. The outlaws had the run of the territory until you came along. And I haven't done much since except count bodies."

Fargo surprised himself by saying, "Don't be so hard on yourself."

"No," Cripdin said. "I should head back east and take up clerking. It's a hell of a lot safer, and the hours are good."

"And you have a better chance of living to old age," Fargo brought up.

"There's that."

They reached Meridian along about eight the next morning and drew rein at the north end of Main Street.

"What the hell?" Cripdin blurted.

Not a single soul was in sight. The street was empty

from end to end. All the doors and every window was shut and not a sound came from any of the homes or businesses.

"It's like a damned ghost town," Cripdin said. "Where is everybody?"

They hadn't gone a block when a door opened and a couple rushed from a house.

"Marshal!" the man hollered. "You should have seen them!"

"It was Cord Blasingame and that breed," the woman said. "They rode in here as brazen as anything."

A flood of townsmen poured from everywhere. They surrounded the marshal, many talking at once.

Fargo was ignored. He hung back and heard enough to get the gist. The two outlaws had appeared with the rising of the sun. The few people out and about had scattered, spreading the word as they went. No one raised a finger, or a gun, as Blasingame and Niyan rode up the middle of the street to the house Glenda rented. No one tried to stop them from going on. No one rushed to help when Glenda was dragged out and thrown on a horse the breed took from in front of the general store. No one intervened when the outlaws left with Glenda and Jennifer.

Fargo's disgust was boundless. He circled the crowd and trotted to the south. He figured the outlaws weren't more than an hour ahead, if that.

It was pushing noon when he saw buzzards. They hadn't descended to feast yet.

She was still alive but there was nothing he could do. The breed had staked her out and gone to work.

Her eyes had been gouged from their sockets but she could hear without ears and she turned her head slightly and croaked, "Who's there?"

"Me," Fargo said. He dropped to a knee and said softly, "Damn."

"Save her," Glenda begged.

"I'll try."

"He's given her to the breed. Can you believe it? She tried to stop them from hurting me. She hit him, and he got mad and said he doesn't care anymore. He said his old life is dead to him, and gave her to Niyan."

Fargo felt his jaw muscles twitch.

Glenda sobbed and tried to sniffle but she didn't have a nose. "Oh God. It won't be long, will it?"

"No," Fargo said.

"It's all my fault. I should have left well enough be. But I couldn't take that he left me. It ate at me." She shuddered and gasped and arched. "Oh!" she cried. "This is my end."

It was.

Fargo left her there. He hadn't gone a mile when he came on Jennifer, fully clothed, her hands on her bosom, looking as sweet and pretty as ever except that her throat had been slit from ear to ear. He left her, too.

Blasingame and the breed had made off to the southeast.

Fargo had a hunch they were leaving the territory. He had other ideas.

Either they were overconfident or they didn't think anyone was after them. They stopped before sundown and got a fire going.

Fargo drew rein well back and waited for dark to fall. He wouldn't chance their slipping away. It had to end. It had to end here.

An owl was hooting when Fargo commenced a silent stalk. He stayed on his belly most of the way, making no more sound than an Apache would. Twice he froze when the breed looked in his direction.

He stopped shy of the firelight. He could drop them then and there but he wanted them to know it was him.

Blasingame was pouring coffee into a tin cup. He leaned back against his saddle and after a long silence said, "I wish you hadn't done that."

The breed was honing his knife. He grunted without

looking up. There was a dark stain on his shirt that hadn't been there before.

"I know she stabbed you, but still," Blasingame said.

"She grab knife," Niyan said. "I not expect."

"She was mad about her mother," Blasingame said. "I can't blame her for that."

"I do what you say to do."

"And you did a good job," Blasingame complimented him. "I was glad to see Glenda suffer after all she cost me."

"Her suffer a lot," Niyan said, and grinned.

Fargo stepped into the light, his hand on his Colt. "Remember me?"

Cord Blasingame froze but not Niyan. The breed whipped his arm back to throw the knife and Fargo drew and shot him in the chest. Niyan fell onto his back but scrambled right back up and lunged for his Spencer. Fargo shot him in the head.

Blasingame still hadn't moved. He stared at the body and said, "Well, now. I never imagined anyone could take him so easy."

Fargo trained the Colt as he went over and picked up Niyan's knife. He came around the fire and squatted in front of Blasingame.

"Gun or blade? Do I get a choice?" Blasingame grinned as if it were funny.

"No," Fargo said.

"I wish she hadn't sent for you."

"Makes two of us." Fargo slashed, just once. The blade bit deep and blood poured.

Cord Blasingame tried to speak but all that came out of his mouth were scarlet bubbles.

Fargo didn't stay. The night wind was cool and refreshing on his face, and promised something better over the horizon.

And, God, he needed a drink.

LOOKING FORWARD!
**The following is the opening
section of the next novel in the exciting
Trailsman series from Signet:**

**TRAILSMAN #378
WYOMING WINTERKILL**

---

*The Rocky Mountains in the winter, 1861—where the cold
and snow . . . and hot lead . . . made for an early grave.*

Wyoming in the winter wasn't for the faint of heart.

Once it turned cold it stayed cold. Not the kind of cold
back east, where a man could throw on a heavy coat and
forget about it. This was a biting cold that froze the mar-
row. The wind made it worse. The temperature might be
ten degrees; the wind made it seem like it was fifty below.

Skye Fargo supposed he should be used to it. He'd been
through Wyoming enough times. But even bundled as he
was in a heavy bearskin coat over his buckskins, he was
cold as hell.

He'd tied his bandanna over his hat and knotted it under
his chin so the wind couldn't whip it from his head. He
could see his breath, and the Ovaro's. Each inhale seared
his lungs with ice so that the simple act of breathing hurt.

Given his druthers, Fargo would rather be anywhere than where he was. But he'd signed on to scout for the army for a spell and the army wanted him to go to Fort Laramie. By his best reckoning he was five days out.

The sky was an ominous gray. Thick clouds pregnant with the promise of snow had yet to unleash their burden.

A winter storm was brewing, and if Fargo was any judge, it would be a bitch.

He hadn't stuck to the main trail. He wanted to get to the fort as quickly as he could so he was cutting overland.

He came to a tributary of the Platte and a crossing he remembered, and drew rein in surprise. He didn't remember a trading post being there. Yet one was on the other side, a long, low building with a crude sign that proclaimed it was run by one George Wilbur and he paid top prices for prime plews. At the bottom, in small letters, it mentioned simply WHISKEY.

Fargo had no great hankering to stop. But half a bottle would warm his innards and ward off the cold for a while when he resumed his ride.

Three horses were at the hitch rail. They looked miserable and he didn't blame them. Only a poor excuse for a human being would leave their animals out in the cold. Especially when around to the side was a lean-to. He dismounted and led the stallion in out of the worst of the wind.

Rubbing his hands, Fargo breathed on his fingers to warm them. When he had some feeling, he shucked his Henry from the saddle scabbard, cradled it in the crook of his left elbow, and walked around to the front door. Before he entered he opened his bearskin coat and slid his right hand underneath and rested it on his Colt.

The rawhide hinges protested with loud creaks.

Welcome warmth washed over him. A fire blazed in a stone fireplace, a pile of wood heaped high beside it.

At the moment a woman of thirty or so was bent over, adding some. She looked around.

So did everyone else.

The place was about what Fargo expected. Log walls, the chinks filled with clay. Rafters overhead. A bar and four tables.

Three men were playing cards; the owners of the horses at the hitch rail, Fargo guessed.

Behind the bar a man in an apron was wiping glasses. He had thick sideburns and a bristly mustache and dark eyes that glittered.

For Fargo, it was distrust at first sight.

The three men didn't inspire brotherly love, either. They were unkempt, their clothes shabby, their coats not much better. Their eyes glittered, too, like wolves sizing up prey.

Fargo wanted that drink. He crossed to the bar and set the Henry down with a loud thunk and swept his coat clear of his holster.

"How do, mister," the barman said. "Cold, ain't it?"

"A bottle," Fargo said. "Monongahela."

"Sure thing." The man turned to a shelf lined with bottles and picked one that hadn't been opened. "I'm George Wilbur, by the way."

"Good for you."

Wilbur opened the bottle and set it down.

As Fargo reached for it he caught his reflection in a dusty mirror. His beard needed a trim and his blue eyes had a piercing intensity that he was told made some uncomfortable. He raised the bottle, admired the amber liquor, and took a long swallow that burned warmth clear to his toes.

"I sell good drinking whiskey," Wilbur boasted.

Fargo grunted. He undid his bandanna and retied it around his neck. The bottle in one hand and his Henry in the other, he walked over near the fireplace and pulled a chair away from a table. He sat so he was partly facing the fire and could keep an eye on the rest of the room's occupants. Leaning his rifle against the chair, he placed the bottle in his lap and held his hands out to the flames.

The woman added another log. She had brown hair and a pear-shaped face that wouldn't be so plain if she gussied up. Her homespun dress couldn't hide her ample bosom and long legs. She gave him a nice smile and turned away.

George Wilbur came over. "Don't say much, do you, friend?"

"Not in this life or any other," Fargo said.

"Eh?"

"Are we friends?"

"Oh," Wilbur said. He shifted his weight from one leg to the other. "I'm just making small talk."

Fargo looked at him.

Wilbur gestured. "We don't get many folks stopping by, is all."

"Makes this a damn stupid spot to build a trading post."

"I make enough to get by and that's what counts," Wilbur said.

Fargo treated himself to another swallow.

"We've got eats if you're hungry," Wilbur said. "The woman here will cook for you. Fifty cents, and all you can eat."

When Fargo didn't say anything, Wilbur coughed and turned and went back behind the bar.

The woman was poking through the wood box. Without looking at him she said quietly, "I'm not a bad cook if I say so myself."

Fargo took another chug.

"My husband, Clyde, got knifed by an Injun when he went out to use the privy and I sort of got stuck here."

"A war party attacked the trading post?" Fargo asked out of mild interest.

"No," the woman said. "There was just the one redskin."

"Only one?"

The woman nodded at the three men playing cards. "That's what they said. One of them is a tracker. He showed me a few scrape marks and told me they were moccasin tracks."

About to take another swallow, Fargo paused with the bottle half tilted. "When was this?"

"Oh, it must have been three weeks ago, or better. About the time the weather turned cold."

"Hell," Fargo said.

The woman turned. "Something the matter?"

"What's your handle?"

"My what?"

"Your name," Fargo said. "And where are you from?"

"Oh. My name is Margaret. Margaret Atwood. I'm from Ohio. My husband and I were on our way to Oregon Country and we got separated from the wagon train and were pretty much lost when we found this place, thank goodness."

"I didn't see a wagon when I rode up."

"Oh. Mr. Wilbur sold it. Seeing as how Clyde was dead, I didn't want to go on to Oregon by my lonesome. So he was kind enough to find a buyer and give me half the money."

"Half?"

"Well, he had to go to a lot of bother. His friends there had to ride to the Oregon Trail and wait for the next wagon train to come along and ask if anyone wanted to buy ours and when no one did they had to wait around for the next."

"Mr. Wilbur was damned generous."

"That's what he said." Margaret grew sad and bowed her head. "I didn't much care, to tell you the truth. With Clyde gone life didn't hardly seem worth living."

Fargo glanced at Wilbur, polishing glasses again, and at the three wolves playing cards. "Son of a bitch."

"Is it me or do you cuss a lot?"

"How many others have stopped here since you came?" Fargo asked.

Margaret knit her brow. "Let me see. There was that traveling parson on his mule. And a drummer. And another wagon with an older couple. They were lost, and Mr. Fletcher"—she pointed at the tallest of the card players—"he's the tracker, he offered to guide them to Fort Laramie. He and his friends were gone about two days."

"Hell," Fargo said again. He told himself it was none of his affair. He didn't know the old couple and he didn't know her.

"Their granddaughter was the sweetest little girl," Margaret remarked.

"How's that again?"

"The old couple. They had their granddaughter with them. Sally, her name was. Her folks got killed in a fire and her grandparents were taking her to live with an uncle who'd settled in the Willamette Valley."

"How old?"

"Sally? She was ten."

The whiskey in Fargo's gut turned bitter.

"Why do you look as if you want to bite someone's head off?"

"Did I hear something about food?"

"Venison," Margaret said with a bob of her chin. "Fletcher shot a buck this morning so the meat is as fresh as can be. I'll whip up potatoes and there are carrots in the root cellar. Would that do?"

"Throw in coffee and you have a deal."

Margaret brightened and stood. "That's fine. And you help me in the bargain."

"I do?"

"Wilbur gives me five cents for every meal I cook for him."

"That much?"

"He's a generous man."

"It's good you're happy," Fargo said.

"I'm lucky to have the work," Margaret replied. "Now you stay put. It shouldn't take me more than twenty minutes or so."

"No hurry," Fargo said. He had some prodding to do first, and it might end in gunplay.

"A writer in the tradition of Louis L'Amour and Zane Grey!" —*Huntsville Times*

National Bestselling Author

RALPH COMPTON

THE BLOODY TRAIL
SHADOW OF THE GUN
DEATH OF A BAD MAN
RIDE THE HARD TRAIL
BLOOD ON THE GALLOWS
THE CONVICT TRAIL
RAWHIDE FLAT
THE BORDER EMPIRE
THE MAN FROM NOWHERE
SIXGUNS AND DOUBLE EAGLES
BOUNTY HUNTER
FATAL JUSTICE
STRYKER'S REVENGE
DEATH OF A HANGMAN
NORTH TO THE SALT FORK
DEATH RIDES A CHESTNUT MARE
RUSTED TIN
THE BURNING RANGE
WHISKEY RIVER
THE LAST MANHUNT
THE AMARILLO TRAIL
SKELETON LODE
STRANGER FROM ABILENE
THE SHADOW OF A NOOSE
THE GHOST OF APACHE CREEK
RIDERS OF JUDGMENT
SLAUGHTER CANYON
DEAD MAN'S RANCH
ONE MAN'S FIRE
THE OMAHA TRAIL
DOWN ON GILA RIVER
BRIMSTONE TRAIL

Available wherever books are sold or at
penguin.com

S543

Frank Leslie

DEAD MAN'S TRAIL

When Yakima Henry is attacked by desperados, a mysterious gunman sends the thieves running. But when Yakima goes to thank his savior, he's found dead—with a large poke of gold amongst his gear.

THE BELLS OF EL DIABLO

A pair of Confederate soldiers go AWOL and head for Denver, where a tale of treasure in Mexico takes them on an adventure.

THE LAST RIDE OF JED STRANGE

Colter Farrow is forced to kill a soldier in self-defense, sending him to Mexico where he helps the wild Bethel Strange find her missing father. But there's an outlaw on their trail, and the next ones to go missing just might be them...

DEAD RIVER KILLER

Bad luck has driven Yakima Henry into the town of Dead River during a severe mountain winter—where Yakima must weather a killer who's hell-bent on making the town as dead as its name.

REVENGE AT HATCHET CREEK

Yakima Henry has been ambushed and badly injured. Luckily, Aubrey Coffin drags him to safety—but as he heals, lawless desperados circle closer to finish the job...

BULLET FOR A HALF-BREED

Yakima Henry won't tolerate incivility toward a lady, especially the former widow Beth Holgate. If her new husband won't stop giving her hell, Yakima may make her a widow all over again.

**Available wherever books are sold or at
penguin.com**

S0096

GRITTY WESTERN ACTION FROM

USA TODAY BESTSELLING AUTHOR
RALPH COTTON

SHOWDOWN AT HOLE-IN-THE-WALL

RIDERS FROM LONG PINES

CROSSING FIRE RIVER

ESCAPE FROM FIRE RIVER

GUN COUNTRY

FIGHTING MEN

HANGING IN WILD WIND

BLACK VALLEY RIDERS

JUSTICE

CITY OF BAD MEN

GUN LAW

SUMMERS' HORSES

JACKPOT RIDGE

LAWMAN FROM NOGALES

SABRE'S EDGE

INCIDENT AT GUNN POINT

MIDNIGHT RIDER

WILDFIRE

LOOKOUT HILL

VALLEY OF THE GUN

BETWEEN HELL AND TEXAS

HIGH WILD DESERT
(COMING APRIL 2013)

Available wherever books are sold or at
penguin.com

S909

Charles G. West

**"THE WEST AS IT REALLY WAS."
—RALPH COMPTON**

Way of the Gun

Even at seventeen years old, Carson Ryan knows
enough about cow herding to realize the crew he's
with is about the worst he's ever seen. They're
taking the long way around to the Montana prairies,
and they're seriously undermanned. They're also a
bunch of murdering cattle rustlers—and now the law
thinks he's one of them...

Also Available
Day of the Wolf
A Man Called Sunday
Death Is the Hunter
Outlaw Pass
Left Hand of the Law
Thunder Over Lolo Pass
Ride the High Range
War Cry

**Available wherever books are sold or at
penguin.com**

S0418

Cameron Judd
Colter's Path

When Jedediah "Jedd" Colter hears of a band of travelers bound for the gold fields of California, he uses his hunting skills to convince the Sadler brothers to hire him as a guard. While the journey is difficult and its leaders incompetent, Jedd's natural skills enable him to keep the peace and save them all from disaster.

But when he's injured along the way and the Sadlers head west without him, Jedd has only one thing on his mind—making it to California on his own and getting even with those that did him wrong…

"Judd is a fine action writer."
—*Publishers Weekly*

Available wherever books are sold or at
penguin.com

S0413